INK
WITCH

Lindsey Fairleigh

Editing by Sarah Kolb-Williams
www.kolbwilliams.com

Cover illustration by Biserka
99designs.com/profiles/biserka

ISBN 978-1539041948

More Books By Lindsey Fairleigh

ECHO WORLD

Echo Trilogy

Echo in Time
Resonance, a novella
Time Anomaly
Dissonance, a novella
Ricochet Through Time

Kat Dubois Chronicles

Ink Witch
Outcast
Underground
Soul Eater
Judgement
Afterlife

ATLANTIS LEGACY

Sacrifice of the Sinners
Legacy of the Lost

THE ENDING SERIES

After The Ending
Into The Fire
Out Of The Ashes
Before The Dawn
The Ending Beginnings
World Before

www.LindseyFairleigh.com

For Greg and the rest of the guys in the shop. Thank you.

Contents

1

"Same question as last time?" I stared across a round table at my Friday night regular, Rita. She was pretty, trendy, and young enough that hanging out in a fortune-teller's studio having her cards read on what was most Seattleites' go-wild night out struck me as a little odd. Especially considering that Rita always asked the same thing: will I fall in love this week? Maybe, but she wouldn't find it in the back of my tattoo parlor, where I moonlighted with my tarot deck. I didn't even need my cards to tell her that.

If I had fifty bucks for every time somebody asked me a variation of the love question . . . well, actually, I did have a fifty for every time, and it more than paid the bills. Nine out of ten clients returned, because I'm that good. Because my cards are legit; made them myself. Because I'm a Nejeret, a god of time. Or a goddess—and I'm really more of a demigoddess, if we're getting technical, descended from the ancient Egyptian god, Re—and my soul is jacked into the time stream. Sort of.

Rita sighed, resting her chin on her palm and tapping the side of her jaw with nails polished a vibrant indigo. "I guess I'm pretty predictable," she said, laughing dryly.

"Only you and the rest of humanity . . ." A species I didn't belong to anymore—hadn't for nearly two decades. I shuffled my hand-drawn deck of tarot cards one more time, then slid it across the pentagram seared into the tabletop. The symbol was purely atmospheric, but clients appreciated the witchy vibe.

"Cut," I told Rita.

She straightened and reached for the deck, picking up a little less than a third and setting it next to the larger stack of cards. "You know, Kat," she said, flashing me a sly smile, crimson lipstick stark against her straight, white teeth, "I've got a good feeling about this reading."

She leaned forward as I retrieved the cards and stacked them to shuffle a few more times. All the shuffling was really for show; the only part of my routine that actually affected the reading was Rita touching the cards. So long as they contacted her skin—her DNA—the spread would fall the same way regardless of whether I shuffled the cards five times or fifty. It's not magic, exactly. Magic doesn't exist, not really. But what I can do—what my people, the Nejerets, can do, tapping into the primal universal energies—is as close of a thing to magic as exists in the real world.

"I've got a good feeling, too," I said, tapping the edge of the cards on the table to straighten out the deck and flashing Rita a quicker, slyer smile. Not that I could actually sense anything from the deck. That wasn't my gift. But Rita didn't know that, and it wouldn't hurt her to have a little faith. My gift lies in the ink itself. Anything I draw has a tendency to take on a life of its own, revealing hidden truths about the past, present, and future, connecting dots that otherwise seemed unrelated.

I set out five cards in a cross formation, then added a column of three cards on the right and one over the center of the cross. And frowned. I'd done this layout thousands of times, but this time it was different. Not because the pattern was strange, but because the designs on the cards were. They'd changed themselves. Again. It hadn't happened in nearly a year, and with the way my life had been plodding along—the definition of predictable—I wasn't expecting the change.

"Is this a new deck?" Rita was craning her neck to look at the cards. She'd been coming to me for six months now, maybe a little longer, and she'd seen every card in the deck at least once. "They look . . ." She tilted her head to the side, eyes squinting. "I don't know . . . darker?"

I shook my head and glanced at her briefly before resuming my study of the cards. "It's the same deck. I just tweaked them a bit." It was a lie. They'd tweaked themselves.

The designs on the cards were actually a reflection of me—of *my* past, present, and future. They'd gone through three major overhauls since I first created them a couple years ago, always when something major was causing upheaval in my life, but they'd been relatively static for the past year or so. Probably because *I'd* been relatively static during that time. It didn't bode well for whatever was to come. I suddenly felt like a live wire, channeling so much sickening dread that my body practically hummed with it. Something would happen, and soon, and there was nothing I could do to stop it.

And there wasn't a single doubt in my mind that it *wouldn't* be a happy something. The cards had taken on an edgier, almost ominous aesthetic. Only heightening the effect was the fact that all of the people depicted on the cards were real people. My family and friends. I hadn't designed the cards that way, and the appearance of familiar faces disturbed me intensely, though I couldn't put my finger on why.

Lex, my half-sister, was depicted as the High Priestess, serene and wise and as unconcerned about the wisps of darkness reaching out for her from one edge of the card as she was about the wisps of light from the other. She also appeared on the Lovers card alongside her husband, Heru. The Hanged Man was my half-brother and mentor in all things lethal and dark, Dominic, all but his pale, haunting face shrouded in shadows.

The only card in the spread that I appeared on was Justice—I was dressed in jeans and a leather jacket, wielding a glowing, crystalline sword in one hand and a golden set of scales in the other.

Disturbed but determined to finish the reading, I focused on the task at hand. Even though the designs on the cards were linked to my soul, the spread—this spread—was all Rita. And there was zero question in my mind that it answered her question. For once, the cards addressed Rita's love life in full.

Sitting back in my chair, the violet, velvet armchair I'd inherited from my mom along with the rest of the shop, I rested my hand on the bulbous ends of the chair's arms and studied Rita's features, trying to gauge her mood. "This is the clearest reading I've done in a long time," I told her. "The cards are split half and half—there's good news, and there's bad news. Which do you want first?"

Rita pursed her lips, then twitched that perfect crimson pucker from left to right and back. "Bad news first." She raised her hand, stopping me before I could start. "No, good news first." She nodded to herself as she leaned forward, placing her elbows on the edge of the table, fingers tangling together. "Good news first," she repeated.

I returned her nod and touched my fingertips to the Two of Cups, then to the Ten of Cups and the Lovers. "These three cards indicate that love is very nearby, and that your partner will make you happier than you ever could've hoped for. This card," I said, touching the Six of Cups, "tells us the person you're destined to be with will be someone you already know, likely someone from your past, possibly even from as far back as your childhood."

"I'm in love with you," Rita blurted before I could warn her that, according to the Three of Swords, Ten of Swords,

Hanged Man, and Justice cards, this person would sweep in to mend her very recently broken heart. Which, apparently, I was about to break.

Well, this is awkward. I shut my mouth, pressing my lips together, and stared at Rita. Her hopeful expression, her flushed cheeks, her bright eyes—this, right here, is why I don't do love. Love is pain and disappointment. It's a blip of joy with a massive hangover of misery. I choose not to feel any of those things, not anymore.

I inhaled slowly, tapping the tips of my fingers in a restrained, steady rhythm on the arm's cutting. "Rita . . . I think we should call it a night. I've got a big job in the morning." A clean break was best. The last thing I wanted to do was give her mixed signals and prolong her agony.

"We could get food, order delivery . . . ?" The hopeful glint in her eyes had faded a little, but she wasn't ready to give up yet. "Or I can cook?"

"Listen, Rita—"

"Is it because I'm a woman? You're not attracted to me?" She was pressing her fingertips into the tabletop so hard that her nails were bleaching of color. "But Jeff at the Goose said he'd seen you leave with both men and women, and I thought, you know, we always have such a nice time on these Friday night dates, and—"

I stiffened. "These aren't dates, Rita." My voice was cold, hard, and Rita flinched at my words. "You make an appointment, you come here, and you pay me for a service." She wasn't the first client to read too much into our relationship—the misperception of friendship, or *more* in Rita's case, was bound to happen when clients shared so much of their personal lives with me—but Rita's profession of love had still taken me by surprise. I was irritated with myself; I was usually better at reading people. Mostly for the sole purpose of avoiding situations like this.

Tears welled in Rita's eyes, spilling over the brim of her eyelids and leaving behind a gray trail of mascara. "But the cards—you said . . ." Her chin trembled, and she covered her mouth with her hand. "Oh God, I've never been so embarrassed in my life."

I scooted my armchair back enough that I could stand. "I'm sorry for that," I said, forcing the words out. I pushed myself up using the armrests and, standing, gathered up the cards. "I'll walk you out." I cleared my throat. "No charge for tonight's reading."

Rita nodded, though she didn't look at me. It was a relief. She slid her chair back and stood.

The tarot studio was in the back of my tattoo parlor, Ninth Life Ink. Back in my mom's day, the place was a retail shop called the Goddess's Blessing selling all things mystical and witchy. But that was years ago, before a war between Nejerets claimed her life, leaving all of her worldly possessions to an eighteen-year-old—me. The Ninth Life had been open for a little over three years now, offering ink to those desiring it and fortunes to those looking for something a little bit more ethereal.

I moved through a heavy beaded curtain of quartz, amethyst, and moonstone that had been around since my mom's time and made my way into the main part of the shop, crystals clanking and Rita sniffling in the background. Rita's kitten heels clacked quietly on the hardwood floor as she followed me across the tattoo shop to the glass front door. I unlocked the deadbolt and opened it for her. She left, head hanging and feet dragging.

"Again, Rita," I said, watching her linger under the covered stoop on the sidewalk outside, "I'm really sorry for the misunderstanding, and I wish you the best. Something good *is* coming your way." *It's just not me,* I thought blandly.

Her head moved in the barest of nods, and she shuffled away.

I shut and locked the door, then wandered around the reception desk to close up shop for the night. I paused to pull out my phone and open my music app, scrolling through playlists until I found one that suited my mood—vintage alternative rock. Some Nirvana, Foo Fighters, and Third Eye Blind was exactly what the doctor ordered. I set the playlist to shuffle and, once the music started blaring over the shop's speakers, closed my eyes and tilted my head back, soaking in the manly angst.

Feeling recharged, I set to work closing out the register. I was just printing out the credit card report for the day when the shop door opened, jingling the little copper bell hanging over the door.

Had I forgotten to lock up after letting Rita out? I was usually pretty good about it when I had after-hours clients, but I'd forgotten a time or two. Except I distinctly remembered turning the deadbolt.

Not that it mattered; there wasn't a lock in the world that could've kept out the man who'd just walked into my shop. He was on the taller side, and athletic, his broad shoulders only emphasized by his long, black leather jacket. His dark brown hair was styled in an undercut, the sides buzzed and the longer top portion combed back loosely. His face belonged to an angel . . . or a fallen angel . . . or a statue of a fallen angel, with all those bold lines, chiseled angles, and that insanely strong jawline covered in a couple days' worth of stubble. A large, brushed silver belt buckle emblazoned with a black Eye of Horus drew my gaze to his trim hips. He was proclaiming his Nejeret clan affiliation pretty boldly with that buckle—Clan Heru all the way. Nobody who knows what they're looking for—and what he is—could miss it.

The intruder stopped a few feet in from the door, his pale blue eyes locked on me. "Hey, Kitty Kat." The corner of his mouth quirked, curving his lips into a confident smirk. "Been a while."

I didn't think. I reacted.

Hands on the counter, I leapt over the top, sliding on my hip until my boots landed on the floor on the other side. I crouched, bending my knees, then sprang at him. I landed one solid smack against his cheek, the force of the hit jarring my whole arm, and then it was a game of striking and blocking, then striking and blocking again. Neither of us held back, and it felt amazing. It had been ages since I'd lost myself in a fight. Too long. Not long enough.

He could've ended it at any time. His brand of "magic" would've allowed him to wrap me up in unbreakable, otherworldly bonds. But the light in his eyes, the vibrancy turning his pale blue irises into burning, gaseous flames, told me he didn't want this to end. Not yet.

He kneed me in the stomach, knocking the wind out of me, then grabbed hold of my ponytail and jerked my head back so he could see my face. "And here I thought you'd be out of practice." His tongue darted out to catch the blood seeping from his broken lip.

"Never," I said through gritted teeth, right before my hand shot out. I gripped his groin through his jeans, fingers viselike.

He grunted, releasing my hair and doubling over. My hand slid off his jeans as he moved, the friction burning the tips of my fingers. Off-balance, I stumbled to one knee.

I pulled myself up with a hand on the edge of the counter. Breathing hard, I straightened my ponytail. "Why are you here, Nik?"

Nik was someone I'd considered an ally a long time ago. Maybe I'd even considered him a friend, but that was before he'd disappeared without a word several years back and nobody had heard from him since. He'd risked his own life to save mine, and then he'd vanished.

I crossed my arms over my chest and glared at him. "Why now?"

Slowly, Nik straightened, wiping the blood from his mouth with the pad of his thumb and giving it a quick, dismissive glance. He'd be healed soon enough—relative immortality was a bonus to being a Nejeret, thanks to our regenerative abilities. It keeps us healthy and young-looking, permanently in the prime of life. In Nik's case, he appeared to be in his mid-twenties. I wasn't so lucky; I would be forever eighteen.

Nik returned my stare, breathing just as hard. "It's Dom—he's missing."

My heart stumbled a few beats at the thought that my half-brother was in some kind of trouble, but I held my head high and redoubled my glaring efforts. "Dom's a big boy," I said. "He can take care of himself." More than—Dominic l'Aragne wasn't just my half-brother; he was also the one who'd trained me. He was one of the most careful and disciplined people I'd ever met, not to mention one of the deadliest. He was also, hands-down, the person I trusted most in the world. If something had happened to him . . .

A seed of dread settled in my stomach. I could feel the roots growing, the branches spreading, the trunk thickening. I balled my hands into fists, appreciating the sting from my nails digging into my palms. Dom was too strong—too smart and skilled—for anything to have happened to him.

"He's been missing for three weeks," Nik said.

That tree of dread spread out, its sickening branches extending into every part of me. But I couldn't accept the possibility that someone could get the better of Dom. The thought disgusted me, and I refused to even consider it. "You were gone for three *years*," I deflected.

Nik shrugged, the motion lazy. "Still would be, but when my mom told me about Dom, well . . ."

My eyes narrowed. "You talked to your mom?" I scoffed and shook my head. "So she found you. Nice of her to tell me you're alive."

Nik's pierced brow arched higher. "The way she tells it, she's been trying to get ahold of you. Maybe if you answered your damn phone every once in a while."

"Well, she could've left a message." I held my glare for a second longer, but shame pushed my gaze down to the floor. I hadn't spoken to his mother, Aset, in over a year. In fact, I hadn't spoken to Dom or Lex or anyone else from our clan in at least that long, and not because they hadn't tried. Though their efforts had certainly waned. They didn't try nearly as hard to get ahold of me as they used to. But after the things I'd done . . . they were better off without me. "I've been busy," I said, fully aware of the lame excuse.

Nik laughed under his breath, then turned, wandering to the nearest open doorway to get a look at the tattoo chair, stool, and desk within the semiprivate room. There were four such "offices" in the shop, each rented out by a different artist, aside from my own private room. This one belonged to a guy named Sampson.

"Yeah," Nik said, walking all the way into the room. "Me

too. I've been real busy."

I rolled my eyes and shook my head. "Fine, whatever," I said, leaning against the counter. "So what's the deal? Why are you here, now? Why are *you* the one telling me about Dom?" So far as I knew, the two had never been close.

"Everybody else is too busy searching for him," he said from within the office. "Which they should've come to you about earlier, except I'm pretty sure they don't know about your little moonlighting gig." He was quiet for a moment. "And I'm not talking about fortune-telling."

My eyebrows rose, and I made my way to Sampson's office. "But *you* do?"

"You find people, Kat. You find people nobody else can."

I stood in the doorway, leaning my shoulder against the doorframe. "How perceptive of you," I said dryly. "How long have you been spying on me?" I was both irritated and flattered at the prospect. But mostly irritated.

"What I can't figure out," Nik said, ignoring my question, "is how you do it."

I wasn't really sure how it worked, either—the magic, so to speak, was in the ink; that was about all I knew. So I gave Nik a dose of his own medicine and ignored his question. "Why hasn't Heru gone after him? Or Mei?" Both were Nejerets with the innate ability to make spatial shifts, and it wasn't beyond their power to focus on a person rather than a place and jump to their target's side in the blink of an eye. Theoretically, either of them should have been able to find Dom by simply thinking about him, then shifting.

Nik glanced at me, elbows folded behind his head. The light from the streetlamps and traffic lights on Broadway shone through the slits of the blinds, making an eerie pattern across Nik's face. "Don't you think they've tried? Dom's not the first Nejeret to go missing. The Senate sent him and a few others out on a mission to find the missing Nejerets—ones even Heru and Mei couldn't find. Mari's among the missing." Mari, my old partner in crime, was as tough as they come. And as powerful.

I swallowed sudden nausea. "Doesn't that mean—" I licked my lips and took a deep breath. "If Heru and Mei can't find them, wouldn't that suggest that they're dead?"

"Most likely," Nik said. "That's what the Senate thinks, at least. But I've been around longer than most of them . . . long enough to know there are limits to our powers. There's always a chance that something is blocking them. I figured it couldn't hurt for you to try, especially since it's Dom . . ."

I crossed my arms once more. "Yeah, okay," I said, nodding. "I'll do it."

2

"You fascinate me, Kitty Kat." Nik gave the shop a quick scan. "When did you become so interesting?"

Those words were funny, coming from him. Real name Nekure, Nik is one of the ancients of our kind. He's I-don't-have-a-clue-how-many thousands of years old and easily the most interesting person *I've* ever met. His mother is Aset, the real-life woman the ancient Egyptian goddess Isis was based on—twin sister to Heru, the real-life man behind the god Horus. Nik's father was some now-dead Nejeret who abducted and raped his mom. I've never heard him given a name.

Nik was the first ever of our kind to be born of two Nejerets—the females of our species are infertile once their immortal traits manifest—and as such, he was born with an additional piece to his soul, a *sheut*, which made him not quite a god, but not just a Nejeret, either. At the time of his birth, he was something new, something more.

All Nejerets are born with a *ba*, the part of our soul that enables us to live forever—so long as we don't get ourselves killed. But not Nik. He was different, the first to be born with a *sheut*, the rare part of a soul that gives its bearer seemingly magical powers. Others came after him—even I had a *sheut* now, a gift from the new gods, who've since abandoned us— but Nik has had the most practice with his, not to mention he played host to one of the old gods in his body for several thousand years.

I have no idea all that he can do with his *sheut*, but I imagine it must be more than he's ever let on. But then, he's never been very open, always hiding behind a wall of sarcasm and smirks. Even when we were close, or close-ish, he'd wielded his attitude like a sword, keeping me at a distance. I was just a young, cursed Nejeret. He was the closest thing left on this earth to a god. I was hardly worth his time, as he'd made so abundantly clear over the years. So how the hell could *I* fascinate *him*?

I stared at the shop's glass door a moment longer, then turned away—from the door and from Nik—and retreated behind the counter to finish the evening tasks. I left the music on as I closed out the register, counting the cash and checks and stashing it all in a zippered bank deposit bag. Somehow, I managed to do it all without looking at Nik despite him watching me from the other side of the counter.

"You grew up," he said.

My heartbeat picked up for a few beats, and I paused in folding up the long credit card report. I couldn't help a quick glance at him. He was just standing there, arms crossed over his chest and pale eyes scrutinizing. I continued folding the receipt tape. "You and I both know *that's* not possible." Thanks to a hasty decision made two decades ago, I was stuck in an eighteen-year-old's body. It was *my* body, always had been and always would be. Teenage hormones and all.

Nik tutted me. "Literal *and* bitter . . . what trick will she do next?"

Closing my eyes, I took a deep breath. While I would never grow into a fully mature adult physically, I was fairly certain Nik's growth was stunted in a much less tangible way. For as long as I'd known him, he'd had the emotional maturity of a frog—and that was probably being harsh. To the frog.

I placed the folded-up credit card receipt into the deposit

bag, tucked it under my arm, and picked up my tarot deck and phone, turning off the music with a tap of my finger. "So . . ." I looked at Nik across the counter. "You delivered your message."

"I did."

I rounded the end of the counter and headed toward the beaded curtain. "Isn't it time for you to disappear?" It was what he was best at.

"I was thinking I'd stick around for a bit," he said. "Maybe help you with the Dom situation."

I clenched my jaw. The last time we'd worked together, it hadn't ended well. "I work alone," I said as I passed through the curtain with a clacking of stone beads and turned to the right, angling toward the door to the stairway that led up to the second-floor apartment.

"Fine." He was following me, practically walking on my heels. "Can I at least crash here tonight? The trip wasn't exactly planned."

I yanked the door to the stairs open. "It's not too late to catch the last ferry. Go stay with your mom on Bainbridge."

"Yeah . . . no."

I stomped up the stairs. "There are hundreds of hotels in this city."

"I'm afraid of bed bugs."

I chuckled without meaning to and caught myself as soon as I noticed I was doing it.

"Kitty Kat . . ."

"Fine," I snapped. "One night. You can sleep on the couch." I twisted the knob of the door at the top of the stairs and pushed it open a few inches, then hesitated. "I, um, don't usually bring people up here." And by usually, I meant *ever*.

Nik leaned in, and when he spoke, his breath tickled the

hairs at the back of my neck. "Lucky me." His voice was low, vibrating with a deep thrum that resonated through me.

My breath caught, and I shivered. "Can you *not* do that?" I said, glancing at him over my shoulder.

"Do what?" he asked, eyes opened wide, innocent as a preacher's daughter.

"Be yourself. Can you just *not?*"

A Cheshire grin spread across his face.

Rolling my eyes, I pushed the door open the rest of the way and walked into the barren living room, noticing things that hadn't stood out to me in years. The only furniture in the room was a couch pushed up against one wall so I had room to move through my daily routine of mixed martial arts poses . . . which had been taught to me by Dom. Several cardboard boxes were piled up against the opposite wall. They'd been there unopened for so long that I no longer had any idea what they contained.

I placed my tarot deck on the kitchen table as I passed it on my way to the hallway. "I'll be right back."

My bedroom was the second doorway on the right—a corner room that had once belonged to my mom. My old bedroom was behind the first door; now it functioned as my personal office, my sanctuary where I experimented with my *sheut* power as well as stored everything relating to the missing persons cases I worked on for private clients. I pulled the door shut all the way as I passed. I didn't want Nik to go in there. I didn't want him in the apartment at all, but I wanted him in *there* least of all.

I stored the deposit bag in the safe in my bedroom closet, swapped my tank top for one not smeared with drying blood from our impromptu scuffle, then headed back out to the living area. Nik was in the kitchen, scoping out the contents of my fridge.

"Eat whatever you want."

"That's easy to say when there's nothing to eat." Nik pulled out a Chinese takeout carton, sniffed it through the closed lid, and gagged. "I'd throw this in the garbage, but I think the smell would stink us out of here," he said, replacing the carton in the fridge.

I pursed my lips, trying to think back to when I'd last had Chinese takeout. Or *any* takeout. I shrugged one shoulder. "There's some frozen pizzas in the freezer. Pick out a couple." I replenished my stock every few days. It was what I lived off of—that and Dick's Drive-In, just a short walk down Broadway. Oftentimes, my trips to grab greasy fast food were the only times I left the shop. All of the teens who worked there knew me by name.

"Maybe you should convert the fridge into a freezer," Nik suggested, head in the actual freezer. "Monthly trip to Costco, and you'd be set . . ."

Fists on hips, I watched him. Or, at least, what I could see of him from behind the freezer door. He'd slung his long, black leather jacket onto the back of one of the kitchen chairs, revealing his array of tattoos in black and varying shades of gray. Our kind healed preternaturally quickly, and as a result, ink didn't stick quite so well in our skin.

Much as I wanted to take full ownership for my own love of the inked needle, I wasn't delusional. Nik had been there when my world fell apart all those years ago. He, and even more so Dom, were the ones who picked up my broken pieces and fitted them back together as best they could. Nik had left an impression. One only needed to look at my choice of business and the ink in my own skin to see that.

"Yeah, maybe." I pulled out a chair and started shuffling

my cards. Habit. "So where've you been, anyway?" Shuffle. "And let me offer up a preemptive *fuck you* for saying, 'Around . . .'"

Nik barked a laugh, pulling his head from the freezer to look at me, those icy eyes glittering with mirth. "Like I said, you grew up, Kitty Kat." The top quarter of him disappeared for another second or two, and then he emerged with two pizza boxes. "Hawaiian and Supreme—two of my favorites."

"Adventurous . . ."

He turned on the oven. "You're the one who bought the pizzas."

I gave him a side nod. "Touché." Was it weird that it felt so *not weird* for him to be there? "So where've you been—really?"

"Everywhere." He tore into one of the boxes. "Nowhere long enough to matter."

"You know, I hated you for leaving like that. After everything . . ." In many ways, I still did.

"I know." That was it, that simple agreement. No apologies, no explanations. Not that I'd expected any. I learned a long time ago that expecting anything from other people was the quickest pathway to disappointment. So I stopped expecting things. No more disappointment.

I huffed a laugh. If only I could do the same with myself.

Nik glanced my way but remained quiet. Good. I wasn't up for sharing my feelings, and I had work to do.

After one last shuffle, I laid out a simple three-card spread—past, present, and future. I didn't need more than that, not with my cards, and not while finding Dom was preeminent in my thoughts. I wasn't surprised to find that the deck had redesigned itself further after the events of the past hour. The illustrations were even more realistic than before, the colors even starker.

The leftmost card represented the past with a row of five crystal tumblers lined up on a barren surface, an ouroboros— a snake eating its own tail—burned into the surface, encircling the cups. Two were shattered, one was broken in half, and the other two remained half filled, one with a clear liquid, the other with something bloodred. Disappointment. Inability to let go. Bitterness. Refusal to give up, to move on. A sliver of hope. The Three of Cups was a depressing card to represent Dom's past. Especially when I knew, deep in my bones, that it was about his past with me.

My eyes burned, but I jutted out my jaw and moved on. The past was the past. I couldn't do anything about it now.

The middle card, representing the present situation, was the King of Swords, reversed. The king sat in his upside-down throne, his massive black claymore planted in the floor at his feet and his head bowed over the pommel, concealing his face. Tyranny. An abuse of power. Deceit. Manipulation. Relentless drive toward a goal. An at-any-cost mentality.

I squinted and picked up the card to get a closer look. There was something engraved into the steel of the sword blade, just above the hilt. "What the hell?" It was another ouroboros, much smaller this time.

"Everything alright?" Nik asked from the kitchen. He was sitting on the counter opposite the oven, watching me. I could see him in my peripheral vision.

"Yeah," I said with barely a glance his way. The self-cannibalizing snake was one of the many ancient symbols my people had used over the years, representing eternity and the cyclical nature of time, but I'd never drawn it on my cards. Why the hell was it showing up now? "Just a . . ." Frowning, I shook my head. "Nothing. It's probably nothing."

"Is this how you do it—tarot cards?"

"Be quiet," I said absently, then moved on to the third card.

The Hanged Man. Again. Goosebumps rose on my skin, starting on my arms and moving inward. The illustration showed Dom dressed all in black and hanging upside down by his ankle. A bright light glowed behind him, illuminating the dark, inky tendrils creeping in all around him, and a snake coiled around his calf, suspended from a branch, holding him in midair. Indecision. Sacrifice. Waiting. Letting go. Surrender. But who—me, or Dom? And why the hell did the snake's tail, once again, disappear into its mouth?

I gathered up the cards and shuffled twice more, then drew three, laying them on the table in a neat row. It was the same cards. One more time—the same spread, the same cards—and I accepted that it was locked in. The universe had spoken.

I settled into a pattern of drawing a single card, a single, specific question in mind.

Where is Dom now?

Did someone capture him?

Is he in pain?

Is he alone?

Who could help me find him?

Is he alive?

Eventually, no matter what I asked, I pulled the same card—the Hanged Man. *Wait,* it seemed to be telling me. *Not yet. You'll understand soon enough.*

Frustrated, I flipped the entire deck over and fanned out the cards. They all had one thing in common—the ouroboros. Sometimes it was hidden, and sometimes it was blatant, but it was always there. I settled into the kitchen chair and started going through the cards one by one. There had to be more they could tell me. There *had* to be.

3

"Why'd you do it?" I ask a hulking Nejeret who calls himself Shank. He's down on his knees, his hate-filled eyes locked on my face, the point of my sword, Mercy, digging into his neck hard enough to draw blood. "Why'd you make him kill himself?"

"Why not?" Shank says. "He was just a human."

I feel my eye twitch, and I'm having a hard time not shoving Mercy's blade forward. That human was my friend. He was helping me. And for that reason alone, this asshat decided to use him as a warning. I grit my teeth. "Give me the names of two others, and I'll let you live." I'm literally lying through my teeth, shame-free. This Nejeret is going to die, regardless of anything he tells me.

Shank smirks, his eyes still locked on mine, and jerks forward. His eyes bulge and his body stiffens as Mercy's blade slides through his neck with almost no resistance.

I raise my right foot and plant the bottom of my boot against his chest, pushing him off the blade. He slumps to the floor, twitching and gurgling as he dies. Preemptive, but no matter. I was going to kill him anyway.

I drop to one knee to wipe the blade off on the side of his sweatshirt.

Shank's eyes are wild now. Scared. Good.

I lean over him and bring my mouth close to his ear. "Don't think this is over." Nejeret souls live forever. If there's a way to make the rest of his existence one of never-ending agony, I'll find it. He's on the top of my shitlist, dead or not, just under the Nejeret who killed my mom.

BANG. BANG. BANG.

I snorted awake, jerking upright in my chair and reflexively wiping the lower half of my face with the back of my hand. It came away wet. Of course.

I could still smell the tangy, metallic scent of blood. I could still hear Shank's final, gurgling breaths. No matter how deserving my victims were of death, they still haunted my dreams.

BANG. BANG. BANG. It was the door downstairs, the one from the street to the shop.

"You should probably get that," Nik said from the couch behind me. "Sounds like a cop knock."

"Oh joy of joys," I grumbled. I pushed my chair back with a screech of wood on wood and stood, blinking gritty eyelids. My cards were still on the table, though not in the neat stack I'd left them in, thanks to my flailing arms. I combed my hair back with my fingers, running my tongue over my teeth in an attempt to decide how terrible my morning breath might be. Pretty bad, I gathered. I felt my chest. At least I was wearing a bra.

I trudged past Nik and the couch, slogged down the stairs, and rubbed my eyes with my left hand as I pushed through the beaded curtain. It was bright, but not full-morning bright. Early-dawn bright. Like, five-in-the-freaking-morning bright. I don't do five in the morning. At least, not from this end.

A large man stood on the other side of the glass door, his physique disturbingly similar to Shank's and his dark blue uniform looking almost black in the pale morning light. Nik, that sneaky charlatan, had been right. Cop knock, indeed.

I unlocked the door and pulled it open a few inches, keeping the toe of my boot wedged behind the door so the guy couldn't shove his way in. I don't have anything against the po-po—they're great, I'm sure. Do-gooders and all that. But I'm not, and that makes us potential adversaries. I have a past that would incite this fresh-faced officer to try to take me in and throw me behind bars without hesitation. Then things would get ugly and he would get dead, and I would feel bad. And really, I wasn't looking to murder one of Seattle's finest at five in the damn morning.

"Is there a problem?" I asked, then cleared my froggy throat. I could hear footsteps on the stairs in the back. Relative immortality, crazy-fast healing, and the occasional "magical" power aren't my kind's only gifts; our senses are extra keen and our reflexes unnaturally quick. I had no doubt that Nik was eavesdropping from the back room. Just in case.

The cop, a Native guy in his mid- to late twenties, nodded to me in greeting. He was quite a bit taller than me and twice as wide—all muscle, from the looks of it. "Morning, miss." He did a quick scan of me, his eyes lingering on the tribal orca tail tattooed on my exposed abdomen, the flock of seagulls flying along my collarbone and over my shoulder, and on the two tiny studs in the snakebite piercings on my lower lip. He glanced over his shoulder, then back at me. "Can I come in?"

I narrowed my eyes. "Why?"

He frowned. "I have an important matter to discuss with, uh . . ." He glanced down at his hand, where my name was scrawled across the palm. "Katarina Dubois. She owns this business, doesn't she?"

I raised one eyebrow. "She does."

"Well, can you get her?" Again, he looked over his shoulder. "Please?" He didn't know enough about me to know that *I* was Katarina Dubois, which told me he wasn't after me for an arrest or anything like that. But he definitely wanted something from me. My help in finding someone, probably. Too bad for him—I only worked for private clients, never for the police. Too many strings.

I flashed him a bright smile. "Sure. Be right back." I shut the door, locking it before turning around to head to the back. I was fully intending to return to the apartment upstairs to continue my investigation into Dom's and the other Nejerets' disappearances. The cards had been stubborn last night, not revealing anything new, no matter how long I studied them. For all intents and purposes, I was in a universe-ordained holding pattern, and it pissed me the hell off.

Nik stepped away from the wall, blocking my passage through the beaded curtain. His eyebrows were drawn together, and the corners of his mouth were turned down. He wanted me to listen to the cop, and he was judging me for planning to ignore the guy. His feelings on the matter were plain as day. Damn it, if Nik was functioning as my moral compass, my own personal Jiminy Cricket, then the world was seriously screwed up.

My shoulders slumped, and I let my head fall back, a groan rumbling up my throat. "Fine."

"Good girl," Nik said, placing his hands on my shoulders and turning me around.

Feet dragging, I headed for the door. I unlocked it and yanked it open. "Come on in." Once the cop was inside, I twisted the lock again and turned to face him, leaning my back against the glass. "Officer . . . ?"

"Smith," he said, pointing to the name tag on his right breast pocket: G. Smith. He craned his neck to peek into the nearest tattooing office. "Officer Garth Smith. Will Ms. Dubois be joining us soon?"

"You're looking at her," Nik said, pushing through the curtain. I glanced past the cop, and my eyes locked with Nik's for the briefest moment. It was like he was allergic to minding his own business.

To Officer Garth Smith, I was sure it looked like Nik was there to intimidate him—it was what Nik did best, after all. But I knew better. He was there for the cop's safety. He probably still thought of me as the loose cannon I'd been two decades ago—the one who'd nearly killed herself in a suicide mission attempting misplaced vengeance for her mother's death. But he didn't know that girl was long gone, killed by an assassin of rogue Nejerets. Killed by me. He didn't know any of that, because he hadn't been around.

"You're Katarina Dubois?" Officer Smith said, spinning around to face me.

I crossed my arms over my chest. "Last I checked."

He did another scan of me, longer than before, from my black combat boots up until, finally, he reached my face. I imagined what he saw—a troubled girl who'd been out partying all night, if the mussed hair, disheveled clothes, and smudged and crusted dark makeup around my eyes were anything to go by.

"You own this place?" he asked dubiously.

"Yep."

"And *you've* been helping people find their missing loved ones for the past two years?"

"Yep."

"But you can't be more than nineteen—"

"I'm older than I look," I said dryly.

His head quirked to the side, his keen eyes narrowed. He thought I was yanking his chain. "How old *are* you?"

"Twenty-five," I lied. I'm thirty-eight, but experience has taught me that telling people anything beyond twenty-five is pushing it. Now, here's to hoping Officer Garth Smith here didn't go look up my actual records . . . then he'd learn the impossible truth. It was probably time for me to start posing as someone new—my own daughter or niece, maybe. But damn that sounded like a lot of work.

"Call it a hunch," I said, "but I'm betting my remarkably good genes aren't the reason you're here."

"Oh, no, of course not, um . . ." Officer Smith shook his head, a surprisingly adorable smile curving his lips. "I've heard rumors—well, more than rumors, really—that you can find people . . . people nobody else has been able to find. I looked back over a few of the cold cases that were solved this past year—always assisted by an anonymous tip." His gaze became hawklike and focused. "It was you, wasn't it?"

Looking to the side, I shrugged.

"The guys whisper about you . . . they say you're a psychic. A real one. Word is you track people through sketches." He inhaled, hesitating with a held breath.

Don't say it. Don't say it. Don't say it.

"They call you the Ink Witch."

I looked past him, to Nik. The ancient Nejeret burst into laughter, almost doubling over.

I glared at him, my hand balling into a fist. "I hate that name," I said under my breath.

Officer Smith looked from me to Nik and back, missing the joke. *I* was the joke.

"You still haven't told me why you're here. I have other things to do . . ." *Other people to find . . .*

"There's a case," Smith said. "Homeless folks have been going missing for a couple months now, but the department can't afford to commit any resources to it."

I cocked a hip and examined my nails. "So, what—you want *me* to solve your missing bums case, pro bono?" We locked gazes. "Out of the goodness of my heart?"

"Well, um . . ." His shoulders drooped; his whole body seemed to deflate. "Yeah."

"Well, um . . . no." I smiled at him, lips pressed together and fake as hell. "Sorry, bud, but I don't work for free." I pushed off from the door, unlocked it, and pulled it open, holding it for Officer Smith.

He headed for the door, pausing when he reached me. His rich, coffee-brown eyes searched mine, his face filled with pleas. "They're kids, mostly. Dozens of them."

My resolve wilted.

"Dom . . ." Nik's voice was barely a whisper, too quiet for Smith's human ears to pick up. I couldn't afford to waste a single ounce of concentration on anything other than finding my half-brother. Not even on missing kids. I had to be ready for the moment the universe decided to throw me a bone and feed me some useful information. If I let myself become distracted by another case, if I let my concentration split, I might miss whatever signal the universe sent my way. Not even poor, missing kids could lure me away from what I had to do.

I hardened my heart and met Smith's desperate eyes. "Best of luck."

4

"So, when you say 'dragon,' are you thinking more *Lord of the Rings* or more traditional Chinese?" I watched my client's puzzled face. "Or something else entirely?" We were sitting in my tattoo office, the one nearest to the back room. I'd chosen it purposefully—anyone who approached the beaded curtain leading to my personal space had to pass by this doorway.

My client looked at his girlfriend for help.

I sat with my sketch pad propped against my upraised knees, pen poised. I just needed some sort of direction for this piece . . . some sort of *anything*. I was down here, working, because there wasn't much else I could do for Dom at the moment. Nik reached out to his mom shortly after Officer Smith left, asking her for a list of all the names of the Nejerets who were missing. With that, I might be able to do some psychic triangulation and finally make some progress. Until then, I had to do *something* to prevent me from losing it completely.

"Well, I mean," the girlfriend started, "we definitely want it to look, you know . . . totally unique."

"Of course," I said, suppressing an eye roll. Maybe working had been a bad idea. I hardly had the patience for this kind of thing right now.

"We were thinking, like, *real*, maybe," the girlfriend said. "Does that make sense? Like, what a dragon *really* looks like."

I was quiet for a few seconds, eyeing them. When neither of their faces gave me any clarity, I said, "But dragons *aren't* real . . .”

The girlfriend waved a manicured hand, her dark green polish contrasting with her almost colorless skin. “You know what I mean.”

I stared at her for a moment, not sure I had the slightest idea what she meant. “Right, so . . .” I looked at my sketch pad and started to draw. “I’m going to sketch out a few possible styles of dragons, and we can go from there.” The last thing I wanted was a bad Yelp review simply because this couple couldn’t describe what they wanted.

The first sketch of a dragon was a pretty crappy attempt, even I could admit that. It was generic and blah. I didn’t even bother showing it to my clients. I flipped the page and started again. The result was something that looked an awful lot like an iguana with tucked-in wings and visible fangs. Pretty damn realistic, if you asked me.

“What about something like this?” I asked, showing them the sketch. “Realistic . . . unique . . .”

The girlfriend bit her lip. “I don’t know . . . I mean, maybe if the wings were open and it had more spiney things?”

I watched the dude’s face as his lady weighed in. “What do *you* think?” He was the one actually getting inked, after all.

He nodded, frowning, just a little. “You know, I’m thinking that maybe it should be bigger—more like something that would be in a world with elves and dwarves and shit like that.”

I bit back a snide re-mentioning of *Lord of the Rings*. “Alright . . .” I sketched out a rough idea. A monstrous, scaly beast with a long, snakelike tail covered in enough spikes to skewer a whole herd’s worth of lamb kabobs, soaring across the page, its enormous wings extended to either side. “So how’s this look to you?” I turned the sketchbook to them.

“Dude, that’s badass,” the guy said.

Smile cautious, I looked at the girlfriend.

"I like it, I guess, but . . ." She scrunched her nose. "Why is its tail in its mouth?"

My eyes opened wide, my eyebrows shooting upwards. I turned the sketchbook my way again, my feet sliding off the edge of the chair. My rubber soles landed on the wood floor with a thump.

The dragon, the sneaky, snakey bastard, had moved. Its back was now curved, its clawed feed tucked in, its wings extended behind it, visible only in profile, and its tail sweeping up to its mouth. Its body, from nose to tail, made a perfect circle. Just like an ouroboros.

I licked my lips, sparing only the briefest glance for my clients before flipping to the previous page. That dragon, the glorified iguana, had twisted itself into an awkward position, its forked tongue extended to reach the tip of its stubbier tail. A quick peek at the first attempt showed me that the lame-o dragon, too, was imitating an ouroboros.

I stood abruptly, hugging the sketch pad to my chest, and muttered a breathy "Excuse me." I hurried to the next office over. Sampson, the only male artist in the shop, sat beside his rented chair, his coil tattoo machine buzzing merrily as he worked on his client's upper back. His coil went quiet, and he looked at me.

"Big piece?" I asked him. I felt hollow, my voice reverberating throughout my entire body.

Sampson nodded. "My whole morning's blocked out for this one." So he wouldn't be able to take over with my clients. "Why?"

"No reason." I forced a smile. "Looks good," I said, barely having glanced at whatever he was working on.

I made a beeline for the counter, where the shop's receptionist was seated on a stool, marking up passages in a textbook
with a pink highlighter. "Hey, Kimi, who's got the least busy
schedule today?"

She closed her book, marking her page with her highlighter, and tapped her tablet's screen, chewing on the inside
of her cheek. "Nobody," she said, looking at me. "We're
booked solid through to close."

I closed my eyes and took a deep breath. This shop was my
life, my livelihood. I *needed* to work. But I needed to find Dom
more. I'd been begging the universe for a sign, for a clue of any
kind. Maybe it had already responded, and I simply hadn't been
listening. That damn tail-eating snake was important. I just had
to figure out why.

"Everything okay?"

I opened my eyes and looked at Kimi. "No, it's not." Even
I could hear the resignation in my voice. "I need you to call
everyone on my calendar today—I have to cancel."

"Oh, no." She pouted her bottom lip. "Are you feeling alright? You do look a little pale."

"I, um . . ." I took a step backward. "I just can't do this
today."

"I can," Nik said, pushing through the beaded curtain.

Both Kimi and I looked at him, eyebrows raised in surprise—Kimi, because she hadn't even known he was there, and
me, because I had no clue that Nik knew the first thing about
giving tattoos; I thought he was just an expert at receiving
them. Kimi's eyes lit with interest as she scanned Nik, and I
could hardly blame her. The guy oozed more bad-boy sex ap-
peal than all of Cap Hill combined.

"Hi." Nik strolled to the counter and held his hand out to
Kimi. "I'm Kat's cousin, Nik."

"We're not related," I said.

"We grew up together."

I snorted. Nik and I couldn't have grown up further apart—his childhood ended thousands of years ago in an oasis in the heart of the Sahara. Mine ended here, some twenty years ago, the day my mom died to save my life. The day Nik dragged me off of her murderer's dead body. The day he watched me come absolutely unhinged.

"I've got years of experience with inking people," Nik said, and my eyes narrowed. People, or just one person—namely, himself? "I'd be more than happy to cover for you if you're not feeling up to it." In other words, *You should be searching for Dom. Why are you even down here trying to work in the first place?*

Because this is the only sane thing in my life, I wanted to scream at him, and I needed a bit of normal to balance out our crazy world. And yet, part of me knew he was right. I'd rather lose this place than lose Dom.

"I just got off the phone with my mom," Nik added. "That information you've been waiting for is upstairs." The list of names of the other missing Nejerets. Finally!

"Yeah? Awesome." I shot a quick glance over my shoulder to where my client and his girlfriend were sitting, heads together as they argued about the style of dragon. "My morning appointments are all consults, but I've got a couple cover-ups this afternoon." I looked at Nik. "Sure you can handle that?"

He grinned. From the spark of mischief in his eyes, I wasn't sure if this was a great idea or a terrible one. It was my business, after all, and I should've cared one way or the other. But I didn't. The hunt for Dom was calling to me through the ink. I had no choice but to answer.

Nejeret is French, technically, derived from a set of ancient Egyptian hieroglyphs—*Netjer-At*—that translate roughly to "god of time." A remnant of where we came from, originally. The universe was dying, and Re, one of the two original old gods, or Netjers, and the co-creator of our universe, along with his partner, Apep, possessed a human just a few moments before birth in the hopes that he could restore universal balance, known as *ma'at* to my people. That human's name was Nuin, and he became the first Nejeret, the father of our species.

Lucky for us all, Re succeeded, and thousands of years after he first came to earth, two new gods were born. And they just happen to be my niece and nephew, Susie and Syris. That's right, my half-sister, Lex, is the mother of the gods . . . but that's another story entirely. The point is, I wouldn't have my special gift, my *sheut*, without those rascally new gods. Of course, I'd probably have a much better idea of what all I could do with my *sheut* if they hadn't gone off to another universe completely to learn how to use their own, much more substantial *sheuts*. So, the new gods and I, we were sort of in the same boat. Or, at least, in the same marina. The one where you go when you don't have any clue about what you're doing. It's a shitty marina. Lots of shipwrecks and flipped boats.

I knelt on the floor of the second, bed-less bedroom in the apartment, surrounded by a ring of sketches. They were all unique, each focusing on a different missing Nejeret, but for one thing—the tail-eating snake. The ouroboros. I couldn't get away from it, not even in my sanctuary.

This room was the only one I actually cared about, the only place I felt at home. At peace. The only place I could be *me*. The only furniture in here was a built-in bookcase covering the entirety of the wall behind me, and I'm not even sure it counted as furniture. Its shelves were filled with a mishmash of trinkets and doodads, of toys and rocks and other little mementos that each had meant enough to someone once that they'd allowed me to forge a connection with that person strong enough that I could find them through the cards and my art. I kept them all, reminders that I could be good. That I didn't always hurt people, that I could help them, too.

One wall, the smallest by the door, was taken up entirely by a closet. That was where I stored my less-savory possessions, the equipment and gear I'd used during my previous, darker career as one of the Senate's deadly hounds alongside Mari. As one of their assassins. It had been more than three years since I'd stowed those tools of death away in there, three years since I'd opened the doors. Had it only been three years? Had it *already* been three years? It felt like yesterday. Like yesterday, and like a lifetime ago.

The other two walls were far from bare. They were covered in black paint as permanent as a mountain, as changeable as a volcano. Like the designs on my tarot cards, the paint on these walls had a tendency to take on a life of its own. It's basically magic, so I don't know why I don't just call it that.

I remembered the way the dragon sketches had changed on their own and felt a flit of panic in my chest. Usually it was only these walls and the tarot cards that reacted so autonomously, along with the odd sketch or tattoo here and there— all things I'd created with intent. With purpose beyond simply existing. All things I'd poured a bit of myself into.

I glanced down at my left arm. The tattoo of the Strength card from the traditional Rider-Waite tarot deck was still there on the inside of my forearm, the lion and the white-robed woman with my mom's face faded almost to obscurity by years of regeneration but otherwise unchanged. There was no sign of a serpent. There was nothing but the tarot card, a reminder of my mom. A reminder of what happens when I care about someone . . . and when I let someone care about me. A reminder to avoid that at any cost.

I blew out a breath. Thankfully, the ink was staying put.

I stared at my latest drawing of Dom. The perspective was strange, as though I was looking down at him from the ceiling. He was standing, looking up at me, and screaming. In pain? In warning? I couldn't tell. I also couldn't tell if I'd drawn something that had already happened, was happening right now, or would happen sometime soon. My gift didn't work like that. I just thought of the person I was trying to find, and if the connection between us was strong enough, my hand started to move.

The ouroboros was in this picture, just like all of the others. It wound around him multiple times before its mouth reached its tail.

"What does it mean?" I whispered. My fingertips traced the sketched lines of Dom's face.

With a splat, a wet spot appeared on the paper, barely missing the snake. I blinked several times and felt my cheek with the fingertips of one hand. It was wet. Because I was crying.

I almost couldn't believe it. I hadn't shed a tear in at least a decade.

Dom's faced changed suddenly. For a few seconds, he wasn't screaming. For those few seconds, it was as though he was actually looking at me through the paper, could actually see me.

"I'm alive," he mouthed. "Find me." I blinked, and he went back to screaming.

"How?" I asked the sketch, voice raised. "Where are you?" I sat up on my knees. Leaned forward, hunching over the drawing. "Dom! Where are you?" I was yelling at a creation of ink and paper, and I didn't care one bit how insane that made me. "How am I supposed to find you?"

I heard the slap of a hand against a wall behind me, then another, and another. Out of the corner of my eye, I could see the paint on the wall bleeding away, pooling near the floor. And still, behind me, the slapping continued.

Until it stopped.

Hand shaking, I set the sheet of paper down on the hardwood floor and climbed to my feet. I turned around and gasped, my fingers migrating up to cover my mouth.

Black hand prints covered the wall in a strip maybe three or four feet off the ground. Small hand prints. *Children's* hand prints.

Eyes wide, I backed out of the room and slammed the door shut. The last thing I wanted was for Nik to stumble across *that* little horror show. I ran into the kitchen and grabbed the tarot cards off the table, stacking them roughly and more or less shoving them into their little drawstring carrying bag.

It was time to pay Officer Garth Smith a little visit and talk about his missing street kids. I was ready to help. Pro fucking bono.

5

According to Officer Smith's card, he was stationed at the Seattle Police Department's East Precinct, right here on Capitol Hill, just a half-dozen blocks southeast of my shop. I didn't even have to take my bike. Not that I ever minded riding the Ducati. But still, how convenient and thoughtful of Officer Smith.

I haven't been in many police stations before, and I'd certainly never been in this one. The building is two stories of whitewashed brick, broad-paned windows, and Tardis-blue trim. I passed under a stoic steel sign proclaiming this the right place and pulled a glass door open. There was a small waiting area to my right—very doctor's office–esque—and a reception window straight ahead. Through the window, I could see several rows of cluttered utilitarian desks, each with a laptop and a phone and a stack of files higher than I thought any one person could get to in a week, let alone a day. Most of the desks were vacant, but a couple were occupied by officers in their blues, neither of which was Officer Smith. The doughy, middle-aged officer watching me peer through the window wasn't him, either.

I spotted Smith standing in the back corner, a coffee cup in one hand and a sugar dispenser in the other, an endless stream of the sweet stuff pouring into his cup of coffee. The man was a damn hummingbird.

I approached the reception window, aware of the stares of the few other people seated in the waiting area. My fitted black leather motorcycle jacket covered the tattoos on my arms, but those peeking out from the top and bottom of my tank top were visible enough. I could practically hear the thoughts whispering through their minds—*troublemaker . . . bad kid . . . keep an eye on her . . .*

I shook my head, laughing under my breath. If only they knew. A quick recount of my personal and professional history could clear a room faster than teargas.

"Fill this out," the heavy, mustached officer at the counter said. The one who'd been watching me. There was the sense of a walrus about him. *C. Henderson*, the name badge on his right breast pocket read. Not knowing what the "C" stood for, I named him Charles in my head, Chuck to those of us who know him especially well.

I glanced down at the form and frowned, then raised my gaze back up to Officer Henderson's face. "Why would I fill that out?"

He coughed, ruffling his mustache. "Aren't you here to report another missing homeless kid?"

"Why would I be doing that?"

Henderson lifted a hand and sort of pointed my way. "You just look the type."

I raised my eyebrows. Homeless kid—that was a new one for me. I slid the form back across the counter to him. "I'm here to see Officer Smith, Garth Smith." Remembering that Garth hadn't seemed too keen on being seen standing outside of my shop, I batted my eyelashes and added, "We have a date." I flashed Henderson a cheeky grin. Maybe I could lend the youthful Officer Smith a little street cred in the process.

"So if you could just skedaddle on over to him there, Chuck-ster, and let him know I'm here, that'd be swell." I sighed. "Isn't he so dreamy?"

Officer Henderson did that coughing, mustache-ruffling thing again, watching me like I'd sprouted two new heads.

I rolled my eyes and leaned to the side to see around Henderson. "Garth," I called out, "I changed my mind about that thing you wanted me to do." I glanced at Henderson and winked.

In the very back of the room, Officer Smith choked on a big gulp of ultra-sweet coffee, his eyes bugging out as he stared at me through the reception window.

I pointed to myself, then to the door beside the reception window, then to myself again, asking without words if I could enter his worktime abode.

Officer Smith, seeming to collect himself a bit, nodded and waved me through. "You can let her in, Charles," he said to Henderson.

I gave a tiny fist pump at my predictive powers. Charles indeed.

Once Henderson opened the door for me, I tucked my hands into my coat pockets and strode into the room. I didn't want anyone mistakenly accusing me of having sticky fingers. I can't count the number of times I've been called a shop-lifter—mostly because I don't care enough to keep track—despite that I've never actually stolen anything. I mean, what kind of monster do they think I am? Stealing—how mundane.

"Can I get you some coffee?" Officer Smith said as I drew near.

I gave his mug a pointed look. "Thanks, but no. I'd like to leave this place with all my teeth intact."

The faintest rosy blush crept up Officer Smith's tan neck.

"Nice place," I said, looking around.

Officer Smith set his mug down on a desk. It had "CHIEF" written on its side in big, bold, black letters. "You're acting like you've never been in a police station before."

I adjusted the strap of my leather messenger bag on my shoulder. "You say that like you assume I have." I tilted my head to the side and smiled sweetly. "I haven't, just FYI. At least, not beyond the waiting area." I pointed to the mug. "You're a little young to be the police chief, aren't you?"

Smith shifted in his chair. "It's a nickname."

"Oh," I said. "Right. It's nice to see that the PD is so PC."

Garth chuckled. "They mean well."

I leaned in and lowered my voice. "So, talk to me about these kids."

Officer Smith exhaled a relieved breath. "I was hoping you'd come around." A hand on my back, he guided me toward the door to the reception area, grabbing a midnight-blue coat off the back of a chair as we passed by. "Let's talk somewhere a little more private."

As we left the station, I gave it an over-the-shoulder scan. All eyes were on us. Either the other cops were super interested in Smith's love life or they hadn't bought my act. Inconceivable, I know.

Smith pointed to a coffee shop across the street from the station, and I nodded. We paused at the corner and waited in awkward silence for the crosswalk signal to change.

Officer Smith seemed a little nervous and fidgety, so I took pity on him. "So . . . how about that local sports team?"

He blew out a breath of laughter, and shallow dimples appeared on his cheeks. "Sorry. I just really wasn't expecting you to come by." He looked at me sidelong. "The guys are going to give me a hard time about that little show you put on in there for weeks."

I flashed him a cheeky smile a moment before the signal changed. I nodded to the other side of the road. "Our turn."

We crossed the street and slipped into the coffee shop just as it started to drizzle outside. I headed for a small two-person table tucked away in the back corner and sat with my back to the wall so I could see everything in the shop. Old habit.

Officer Smith sat in the chair opposite me and leaned forward, resting his elbows on the table. "So, what changed your mind about helping?"

"I'm a bleeding heart." I pulled back the flap on my bag to dig out my cards. I paused, the deck's drawstring bag partially exposed. The bag was made of a midnight crushed velvet, an Eye of Horus embroidered in silver thread on one side, an Egyptian-style cat on the other. The first was a symbol of my Nejeret clan, changed from my clan of birth—the Set clan—to the Heru clan via an oath. The other I thought pretty obvious: cat . . . Kat.

I looked from the cards' bag to Officer Smith and back, squinting thoughtfully while I tugged on the inside of one of my lip piercings with my teeth. I returned to looking at Smith. "Would you consider yourself a superstitious man? Like, on a scale of one to ten, how open would you say you are to things like, say, *magic*?"

"Which end is which?"

"Ten is 'I wish I could do that,' and one is 'burn them all.'"

"I don't know . . ." Smith scratched his jaw. "I was raised in Seattle, but I spent summers back on the Squamish reservation with my people, learning our traditions and whatnot. I think a lot of folks would say there's some magic in that."

"Well, alright," I said, mildly impressed. It didn't happen often.

I pulled the tarot cards out of their little drawstring bag and started shuffling. "So, officially, I'm a tattoo artist and a fortune-teller. Finding people"—I tapped the two halves of the deck on the tabletop, then shuffled once more—"that's just an extension of the fortune-telling gig. I'll do a reading for you here, but the rest of what I do . . . that happens behind locked doors. I'm going to need everything you have on the missing kids. The more accurate your information is, the more accurate mine'll be." I paused, glancing at Smith. "I don't suppose you have anything that belongs to any of these kids?"

He shook his head. "Do you need that to make this work? Because I know where some of the kids were bunking down. We can go by in a little bit and—"

I raised a hand, cutting him off. "Thanks—I appreciate it, really—but no. I work alone." I gave the cards one last shuffle, then slid the deck across the table to him. "Just give me the info and I'll take it from there." When Smith didn't do anything, just sat there, I glanced down at the deck pointedly. "Cut it, please. And while you do, think about this case, these kids . . . how much it means to you to find them."

Smith's brow furrowed as he concentrated. He was actually taking this seriously, which was both a pleasant surprise and a welcome relief. He looked at the deck like he was trying to set it on fire with his stare alone, then finally cut it, dividing it almost perfectly in half. "Just the once?" he asked, eyes on me.

I nodded and reached across the table to retrieve the deck. I opted for a simple three-card spread to start off, wanting to ease Smith into my brand of divination.

Once the cards were laid, there was no ignoring the fact that the deck had altered itself once more. I wasn't surprised this time. Of the three cards—the Five of Pentacles, a card representing poverty and insecurity, the Eight of Swords, representing isolation or even imprisonment, and the Tower, representing disaster, upheaval, and sudden change—two displayed a person, and each was a child. Both children displayed were strikingly different. It didn't slip past me that Dom was the man tumbling out of the crumbling tower, but for the briefest moment, all I could think about was the children.

"How many kids have gone missing?" I asked. "That you know of, at least?"

"Seventeen have been reported missing by their friends, all in the last two months."

I flipped the deck over and skimmed through the rest of the cards, double-checking what I felt in my gut—the major arcana cards like the Tower all still depicted Nejerets, but each and every figure of a person on the minor arcana cards, like the trio of girls on the Three of Cups, had transformed into a child, and each one was unique. Instinct told me I was looking at the faces of the missing kids.

"Seventeen," I said quietly, shaking my head as I counted the children. "That's not all of them." *Thirty-two . . . thirty-three . . . thirty-four . . .* "There are thirty-five kids missing, total," I said, finally setting the deck down.

Smith leaned forward, craning his neck to get a better look at the cards. "And the cards told you that?"

"Sort of." I didn't explain how it worked, partly because I didn't understand it fully myself, but mostly because he wouldn't understand *at all*. Smith was open-minded, and that was almost more dangerous than a skeptic. If I shared with him how I knew there were thirty-five missing kids, he'd want me to explain how it worked. He'd want me to explain everything. And then I would have to get rid of him, because, in the case of my people, sharing is *not* caring. The Senate had a strict policy on not telling humans about our existence. It used to be allowable to share with parents, spouses, and children, but the Senate had tightened up the policy of the past few years to be explicitly "No humans allowed."

When Smith opened his mouth and inhaled, preparing to dig further, I cut him off with a raised hand. "I won't tell you more. I'm sorry, but I can't." I met his rich brown eyes. "It's for your own good, trust me."

He shut his mouth. Smart man.

"Officer Smith—"

"Garth, please."

I nodded. "Garth, does this symbol mean anything to you?" I asked, tapping one of the snakes on the Five of Pentacles card. The external circle of each pentacle was an ouroboros.

Garth leaned over the table to get a better look at the card and the symbol I was pointing to. "Can't say it means anything to me, personally."

I huffed out a breath and drummed my nails on the tabletop, staring at the tail-eating snake. Why did the damn thing keep showing up?

"But," Garth continued, "I'd guess there isn't a person in this country who wouldn't recognize it these days."

My eyes snapped to his. "Why?"

"That's the logo for that company that's making Amrita. I swear their commercial is on between every show on TV."

"I don't have a TV," I told him. "What's 'Amrita'?"

Garth's eyes rounded, like he just couldn't believe I didn't turn into a couch zombie along with the rest of America every evening. "Amrita—the elixir of life. You know, the one that claims it can add another fifty years to your life." His eyebrows climbed up his forehead. "You've really never heard of it? It's on billboards and the sides of buses . . . in magazines . . ."

I shook my head. "Not ringing any bells, but then, I don't get out much. So what's this drug company called?" I pulled out my phone and opened the Internet app. "And how do you spell 'Amrita'?"

Garth told me, then shook his head slowly, his eyes squinted in thought. "I can't remember the company's name. It's something strange . . . definitely not an English word. Might be Latin."

My phone was working at a slug's pace, but I didn't need it anymore anyway. I set it down and looked at Garth, a strong hunch perching on my tongue.

He frowned. "I think it starts with an *O*."

"Ouroboros," I said, letting that hunch fly free.

Garth snapped his fingers. "That's it. The Ouroboros Corporation."

I bolted up out of my chair, adrenaline coursing through my veins. I stuffed my cards back into their little drawstring purse and tucked them away in my messenger bag, then slung the strap over my shoulder, a genuine smile curving my lips for the first time since Nik arrived. Dom was alive, his disappearance was linked to the missing kids, and it all had something to do with this Ouroboros Corporation.

Finally, I had something to go on. A sleazy pharmaceuticals company that specialized in life-extension drugs; it was about as solid of a lead as I could've asked for.

"Thanks, Garth," I said, standing beside the table and looking down at him. "This has been insanely helpful."

"What—where are you going?"

I turned away and started across the coffee shop toward the door. "To track down your missing kids." I glanced back at him. "I hope you're not a fan of that corporation. They're involved in this somehow, and I *will* burn them to the ground."

Garth blanched.

I winked at him. "Figuratively, of course."

Once I was out of the room, I uncrossed my fingers. If Dom was hurt in any way, I would stop at nothing to destroy them.

6

I tossed back the remaining bourbon and thunked my glass down on the kitchen table beside my laptop, already reaching for the bottle. My eyes never left the computer screen. The rest of the apartment was a dark cavern compared to the glow from the screen. Afternoon had come and gone in the blink of an eye and the click of a mouse, and evening had fallen. Nik was still downstairs, working in my place, and I'd been alone in the apartment, barely having moved since getting back hours ago. I couldn't, not when my eyes were glued to the screen.

I checked my inbox for the bazillionth time—I'd emailed Garth as soon as I got home, reminding him to send me the info on the missing kids—before maximizing the browser window again. I now knew pretty much all there was to know about the Ouroboros Corporation. At least, everything available to the public.

Ouroboros is the pharmaceutical arm of a multibillion-dollar global conglomerate called Initiative Industries, which owns subsidiaries in all branches of industry and commerce. Ouroboros focuses on what they call "life-extension technology and therapy." In other words, they're looking for the fountain of youth—eternal life—something they can cram into a pill and bottle up.

Funny. Nejerets *have* eternal life. At least, so long as we don't get ourselves killed. There was zero chance that those two facts weren't linked, and that left little doubt in my mind that the missing Nejerets hadn't just been abducted for shits and giggles, they were being experimented on. Apparently, right alongside the missing street kids. These Ouroboros people were their own special brand of sick fucks.

I took a sip from the fresh glass of bourbon, thoughts of grim reapers dancing through my mind. I would find them, and I would hurt them. It's what I did best, even if I was retired. This was worth getting back in the game for.

I'd moved on to reading reviews of some of their products. The most elite was Amrita, a series of injections given weekly for one year, but there wasn't much information about what the injections actually did, other than "rejuvenate the body and soul," let alone a price tag. The most popular product seemed to be Amrita Oral, a pill taken twice daily for some undisclosed period of time that was purported to slow the aging process through metabolic and adrenal regulations. It was pricey, though they offered the first month free for anyone who visited one of their many nationwide open houses. They held them weekly in New York City, Boston, Chicago, Dallas, Los Angeles, San Francisco, and—what do you know—Seattle.

Their Seattle open house was every Sunday morning at ten thirty at their corporate headquarters downtown. It was Saturday night. The next one was tomorrow.

I clicked back to the official website and started filling out the registration form, a requirement to attend. First and last name—I went with Katherine Derby. Date of birth—I shaved off a decade and a half there. Email—easy enough to create a new account for Ms. Katherine Derby. Phone—I hesitated here, not willing to enter the numbers for my cell or the shop phone.

I stood and went into the kitchen, opening the drawer

where I used to keep a stash of unopened burner phones back during my former, illicit career. Although, technically, I *had* been licensed to kill by the Senate, it still felt like my sixteen years as one of their leashed assassins was about as wrong as a thing could be. All of the old burners were gone, leaving just one antiquated cell phone in the drawer—my mom's old phone.

I picked it up and pressed the power button, knowing full well the battery had died eons ago. Nothing happened. But even though the phone was kaput, the line wasn't. I'd purchased the rights to both her and my cell phone numbers seventeen years ago, just after the bill legalizing the universal privatization of all forms of "intangible property" passed in Congress. I grinned. When I'd purchased her line, I'd registered it to her—Genevieve Dubois—not to me. It was perfect.

I swapped out her name for my hastily created pseudonym, signed her up for a brand-spanking-new email address, and typed in her phone number. My pointer hovered over the *REGISTER* button. I'd made it this far at least a dozen times so far, using a dozen different identities. *Don't be a moron,* my brain screamed. *It's too risky—I'm a Nejeret; they're abducting Nejerets . . .*

The apartment door opened, and Nik walked in.

I clicked the register button reflexively, then closed out the window. Decision made. I was going.

I gulped down half the glass of bourbon and slid the bottle toward Nik as he neared the table. "Drink?"

Stopping to stand at the end of table, he spun the bottle around and whistled. "You might be a culinary prude, but your taste in booze doesn't suck."

I snorted a laugh, my gaze trailing down the length of his body. He looked damn good right now. It was the alcohol, I knew it, but I couldn't stop myself from appreciating his appearance. Tall and lean. Athletic, but not bulky. His thin, faded black T-shirt just snug enough to show some muscle definition across his chest and shoulders. The front hem of his shirt tucked precariously into his jeans, showing off his silver Eye of Horus belt buckle. The black and graying ink staining his arms and neck. I thought his neck piece—a tattoo of the goddess Isis, kneeling, her extended wings wrapping around to the back of his neck—just might be my favorite. At least, of the ones I could see. Who knew what was under his shirt—my eyes traveled lower—and elsewhere. But that Isis tattoo was similar to something I'd been planning for my forearm for a damn long time.

And then there was his face, all pristine, hard lines and sharp edges. It was perfectly symmetrical except for a slight bend in his nose where he must've broken it and been too slow to reset it before it healed. He could still fix it easily, if a little painfully. But then, Nik had never shied away from pain. Rather, so far as I remembered, he reveled in it.

His dark eyelashes and brows contrasted with his eyes, making his pale blue irises stand out even more, icy and calculating. There was nothing soft or warm about Nik. Especially not the way he was watching me study him.

"See something you like?" he asked, his striking gaze locking with mine. There was heat in his stare. Heat, and a challenge. I wondered what would happen if I told him, "Yes." Something, I felt certain. But what? It was impossible to predict.

I cleared my throat and took another sip of bourbon. "Professional admiration," I lied. "I like the neck piece. Who did that one?"

"Someone in Anchorage," he said, his expression blank,

his eyes anything but.

"A woman?" I asked without thinking.

The corner of his mouth quirked, hinting at his usual smirk. "Why?"

I shrugged. "How long did you have to sit for it?"

"Six hours," he said, a knowing glint in his eyes.

I licked my lips. "Just, um, one session?"

He nodded and turned to head into the kitchen.

"How much did she charge?"

Nik grabbed a glass from the nearest cupboard and returned to the table to pour himself a drink. "I didn't pay her in money," he said, glancing at me, more than a hint of a smirk now.

I tried my hardest not to react, but damn it, I could feel the traitorous blood heating my neck and cheeks. I lowered my gaze to stare at the bottle across the table and cleared my throat. "Where are you staying tonight?"

Nik chuckled, low and quiet, and my stomach did a little flip-flop that wasn't entirely unpleasant.

I spluttered my bourbon. "I didn't mean—" I stood partway and reached for the bottle. "You know what I meant," I said, not quite sure that I knew what I meant.

Nik's stare burned into me for a moment longer. "Sure, Kitty Kat. I know what you meant." He turned and walked back into the kitchen. "I was hoping to crash here again—payment for a day's work." He opened the fridge, shook his head, then opened the freezer. "Pizza?"

I watched him for a moment, gathering my scattered wits. "You don't want to go back to Bainbridge, do you?"

Bainbridge Island was the current territorial base of Clan Heru. Heru ruled over the entire Pacific Northwest, including Northern California from San Francisco up, extending all the way to Alaska. He owned the entire northern quarter of Bainbridge, where he, Lex, and their daughter, Jane, lived with several dozen other Nejerets. Nik's mother, Aset, was among them. Hundreds of others passed through each year, as it was required for Nejerets from other clans to request permission and receive a license of passage *or* residency, depending on their intended length of stay in his territory.

Nik was quiet for a few seconds, his head in the freezer and the rest of him unmoving. I took it as an opportunity to ogle a bit longer. "They don't know I'm here," he finally said.

I blinked, surprised. "But you talked to your mom and—"

"I didn't tell her I was actually coming back here to help with the search." He pulled two frozen pizzas from the freezer. "Just that I'd look into it."

"So nobody knows you've involved me, either?"

He shrugged one shoulder, then turned on the oven. "Who's to say the Senate's not involved in the disappearances?" He tore into one of the boxes. "It's better for us both if nobody knows I'm here."

"Except for me," I said quietly.

Nik looked at me, the tiniest smile curving his lips.

My heartrate picked up, and I broke our stare, focusing instead on my empty glass. "You can stay." I lifted one shoulder. "It's only fair, with you filling in downstairs . . ."

He grunted a thanks. "So what've you found?"

"Hmmm?" About Dom. Right. "Oh, um, it looks like the missing Nejerets are linked to other disappearances. A bunch of homeless kids have vanished from the area as well."

"What that cop came to you about this morning?"

"Garth, yeah." I nodded and refreshed my inbox, using the computer screen as a way to avoid eye contact with Nik. "I'm just waiting for some files from him right now. Until I get those, I'm in a holding pattern . . ." I purposely didn't tell Nik about Ouroboros. He was barely involved in this as is, aside from playing messenger, and I didn't want to suck him in further. He still had people who would be devastated if he died, his mother, first and foremost. I respected Aset too much to get her only son killed. And then there was me . . .

"No plans for the night, then?"

I raised my eyebrows. "None that I'm aware of." I laughed to myself. Really, did I *ever* have plans for the night? For *any* night?

Nik hoisted himself up onto the counter, where he sat, boots dangling. "I could use a few touch-ups. We could trade . . ."

Frowning, I nodded. As far as ideas went, it didn't suck. Besides, I relished the chance to get a peek under his shirt—professional curiosity, of course. "Let's eat," I said, "then head down to my office." I was already thinking about what I'd have him work on. I always had a gang of tattoos in the lineup. Unlike Nik, I didn't just trace over my already-existing pieces, refreshing a static pattern. I liked to change it up. When one piece was faded enough, I just inked something new over the top.

I laid off the bourbon while we ate, and by the time we'd polished off the pizza, I was sober as a stone. Some might see it as a perk, but the metabolism that comes hand in hand with Nejeret healing can be the most annoying of burdens. When we need to eat, we *need* to eat. If we don't, our regenerative ability will turn off until it has enough energy to fuel it, and we start aging or losing weight—rapidly. It's the only way I'll ever look any older than my physical eighteen years, however temporarily. On the plus side, our metabolisms also enable us to process alcohol insanely quickly. I could be ass drunk one hour, dead sober the next.

"Alright," I asked Nik as he followed me into my private tattooing office. I flicked on the light switch on the wall, then turned on a secondary lamp. "What am I touching up first?"

He tugged his shirt off over his head, and I stared without blinking. His entire torso was a mass of black and graying ink over taut skin and hard muscles. It was chaotic and beautiful and impossible to take in completely in just a few seconds. I licked my lips, swallowing roughly as my heart rate escalated once more. So maybe it hadn't been the alcohol fueling my attraction to him upstairs. Clearly, I needed to get laid.

Nik seemed oblivious to this round of gawking. "My left rib piece is probably the worst," he said, lifting his arm and craning his neck to get a better look. "It's nothing complicated—just a list of names."

"I can see that," I said, leaning in close and breathing softly. He smelled amazing—clean and fresh, with just a hint of something spicy and ancient that reminded me of the incense my mom used to peddle in this very shop. Aroused didn't even come close to how I was feeling. "Only, um, a few of the names are in English."

Nik laid on his back on the narrow, padded bed. "Well, since English didn't exist for most of my life . . ."

"Right. That makes sense." I turned away from him and started gathering up my tools, impressed by how tidily he'd worked in my space. "So, who are they? Or *were* they? People you cared about? Or people you killed?" I asked, projecting with that last guess. That was the list of names I'd ink into my own skin. It was a long list.

"Something like that." Nik's voice sounded distant.

"Sorry." I set the ink and tattoo machine on a rolling table, along with a fresh needle and a few sanitizing wipes. "Didn't mean to pry. So, why only black ink?" I'd never seen him with anything else.

Nik laughed under his breath. "I tried color once, back in the forties—didn't like the look of it as it faded."

I could relate. I only rarely incorporated color into my own tattoos, and even then, only as accents.

"But I do have one piece that isn't done in black ink," Nik said, rolling onto his side.

I sucked in a breath. "Holy shit . . ."

Nearly his entire back, from his broad shoulders down to his trim waist, was a cascade of hieroglyphs done in some impossible iridescent ink. It shimmered in the light, making his skin look like it had been inlaid with mother-of-pearl.

"Is that—"

"*At?*" he said. "Yeah. Made the ink myself."

At was one of the two energies that made up everything in the universe. All of space and time was held together by *At* and its counterpart, what I'd dubbed *anti-At*. The closest human science has come to capturing the truth of things is through particle physics, with matter and antimatter. That's the closest humans have come to understanding the universe—and it's not very close at all.

For thousands of years, my people were gifted with the ability to leave our bodies and enter a higher plane of existence, one where those primal forces are visible as a swirling, rainbow miasma of the fabric of time and space. There, we'd been able to view almost any time, any place, from that other plane in what we'd called echoes. The echoes were closed to us now, had been for over three years, ever since the new gods abandoned us.

Nik had the unique innate ability to pull one of those otherworldly forces, *At*, into our physical plane of existence, courtesy of his *sheut*, his internal, magical power source. He was the only person alive who could do it, and there was just one person in the world who could do the same with *anti-At*—Mari, my old partner in crime—though her abilities were far more limited. And way more dangerous. A single touch of obsidian-like *anti-At* could unmake a Nejeret from the *ba* out, erasing their poor, dwindling soul from the timeline completely until it was as though they'd never existed at all.

At, however, was different. Touching it wouldn't harm a person, and Nik's control over it was mind-blowing. He could make virtually anything out of the otherworldly material, including the sword stashed away upstairs in my closet with the rest of my forgotten assassin's gear. He could create whole buildings out of *At* or restrain someone in seemingly living vines of *At* or turn an entire person into *At*, either to preserve or punish. Apparently he could make tattoo ink, as well.

"It's the only way I've found to make a permanent tattoo," he explained. "For us, I mean."

I licked my lips. "Would you make me some of that ink?"

"Yeah, sure, Kitty Kat." He extended his arm over his head in preparation for me to begin working. "Whatever you want. All you have to do is ask."

7

The Ouroboros corporate headquarters were housed in the tallest building in Seattle, the Columbia Center. The skyscraper was intimidating for more than its height—it was a dark giant, an immense structure with an exterior as black and reflective as fresh-cut obsidian that took up an entire city block. The ground floor consisted of an expansive and varied food court, the second by a mall's worth of shops. I may have stopped at the coffee shop near the entrance for a couple of donuts—a maple bar and an old fashioned—and a black coffee on my way in. Aaaaand I may have scarfed down both pastries by the time the escalator carried me up to the second floor, the lowest level reached by the elevator.

There was a sign at the top of the escalator advertising the Ouroboros open house, proclaiming that it was today, on the sixtieth floor. And would you look at that—they *hope to see me there!* So friendly, these evil, kidnapping, child-torturing corporate scientists . . .

I rode the elevator up with a handful of people of various ages. A man and a woman in their thirties stepped off on floor eighteen, chatting about people in their office, and an older, dignified woman in a tailored skirt suit left on floor forty-one, leaving me with a middle-aged man and a younger couple. We all rode to the sixtieth floor.

When the elevator dinged and the doors slid open, I hung

back, scoping out the scene. A couple of greeters waited a dozen or so steps out of the elevator. Both were attractive men in the prime of youth, wearing identical gray slacks and navy blue button-down shirts. Nice subliminal advertising, these handsome, youthful fellas. They latched onto my elevator companions, leaving me to slink out unnoticed.

I'd like to point out that I even dressed for the occasion. I was wearing my nicest jeans—dark and totally hole-free—the one and only turtleneck I owned, and a charcoal-gray hooded trench coat, tied at the waist. I'd swapped out my usual combat boots for some black leather riding-style boots, and I'd even removed my lip piercings. By the time I returned home, the damn holes will probably have closed up already, which was a pain in the ass. I looked downright respectable . . . at least, to these kinds of people. But I *felt* ridiculous. Anybody from the shop would've spit out their coffee if they'd seen me like this. Which was precisely why I'd slipped out the back door.

The shimmering tip of my brand-new tattoo—an image of the goddess Isis very similar to the one on Nik's neck, with the exception that *this* goddess bore a striking resemblance to my mom—peeked out from the end of my sleeve onto the back of my hand. All other tattoo ideas had gone out the window as soon as I'd seen the *At* ink piece on Nik's back. I tugged at my sleeve as I walked across the lobby, hoping nobody noticed. It didn't really strike me as the tattoo kind of place.

"Miss!" someone called after me. "Excuse me!" Fast footsteps carried the voice closer, and a third young man dressed just like the other greeters in gray slacks and a blue button-down shirt jogged my way. "Are you here for the open house?"

"Yes," I said, splashing on a broad smile and airhead eyes. I blinked several times and pretended to scan my surroundings. "Am I going the wrong way?"

"No, but you do have to check in." His brow furrowed. "Did you register online?"

"Of course I did," I said, touching my fingertips to his forearm and meeting his eyes. "I *can* follow instructions . . . when I want to." I gave him a wink. Too much?

"Great!" He pulled a sleek little smartphone from his pocket and traced a circle on the screen. "Name?" he asked, looking at me.

"Gen," I said. "Genevieve Dubois. I just registered last night—it was sort of last minute." I put on a worried expression. "I hope that's okay . . ."

"Yep," he said cheerily. "I see your registration right here." He held his arm out, telling me to head toward the single open door on the left side of the lobby, where a table was set up with name badges and a fanned-out stack of navy blue folders with the tail-eating snake emblazoned on the front in metallic silver. Two women manned the table, one in the increasingly familiar dark gray and blue—I was sensing a color scheme—the other wearing a smart black pencil skirt and a cream blouse.

"Candace will finish checking you in," my greeter said, handing me off to the uniformed woman. "And lucky you, Ms. Dubois, you can meet one of the Amrita leads, Dr. Marie Jones."

I glanced at the non-uniformed woman and froze. She was no "Marie Jones"; her name was Mari. She was *my* Mari—my ex-partner in assassinating the Senate's enemies. The same one whose name had been counted among the missing Nejerets. Things hadn't ended well between us, what with her calling me a coward the last time I'd seen her and me flipping her the bird. But we'd had some good times . . . and some dark times. Regardless of our past, or maybe because of it, I was genuinely glad to see her. At least I now knew that she wasn't one of the victims.

Then, dread sprouted in my belly. If she wasn't one of the victims, why was she here?

"Ms. Dubois," Mari said, extending her hand. She looked awesome. Her sleek, short inverted bob offset her Japanese features beautifully, and her brilliant jade-green eyes had never been more striking. "A pleasure to meet you." She grinned woodenly. "What brings you to our open house today? You couldn't be a day over eighteen."

I shook her hand, narrowing my eyes minutely. What game was she playing? "Twenty-five, actually. And it's never too early to start planning for the future, at least that's what my mom's best friend Mei always said." Mei was a Senate member and the leader of her own clan, occupying the Great Plains territory. But more importantly, she was Mari's adoptive mother.

Mari's cheek twitched. "How fascinating. Please"—she gestured for me to step off to the side with her—"chat with me for a moment. Yours is a demographic we've yet to really reach, and I'd love to get your input on a few ideas."

I matched her, wooden grin for wooden grin. "Love to."

Mari led me to a cluster of chairs in a corner of the lobby about as far as we could get from the check-in table and the elevator. "Just keep smiling pleasantly," she said through clenched teeth as she smoothed down the back of her skirt and sat.

I did as requested, sitting in the chair beside hers and angling my knees her way. "What the fuck are you doing here, Mars?" I asked through gritted teeth.

Her jade eyes flashed with irritation. "I should be the one asking you that. Did the Senate send you?"

I shook my head, stupid smile plastered in place. "Nik showed up and told me that a bunch of Nejerets are missing.

It's looking like this place—you guys—are involved. But no, the Senate didn't send me." I laughed under my breath. "I'm sure the Senators would shit their collective pants if they knew I was here."

Mari leaned in a little. "Nik's back? I thought nobody had seen or heard from him for years."

"They hadn't," I said, not bothering to tell her that he'd been in contact with his mom. "Mari, what are you doing here?"

"The Senate sent me in undercover about six months ago because they thought the corporation's research was suspicious. I was just supposed to blend in . . . to monitor. But a couple months ago, when I heard about some of our people going missing, I started to actively investigate."

It was my turn to lean in, elbows on my knees. "What did you find? Do you know where Dom is? Is he still alive?"

Mari's eyes widened, her smile faltering. "Dom's missing, too?" She shook her head, a crease forming between her eyebrows.

"You didn't know?"

"Smile," she reminded me. "And no, I had no clue about Dom. The most I've been able to find out is that there's some sort of a shipment that goes out every couple nights—one that's off the books. It *might* have something to do with all of this, but . . ." She shrugged. "It's weak, at best. I tell you what—one of those shipments is going out tonight. Why don't I text you the address and you and Nik can check it out? I'll snoop around here to see what else I can find out and contact you in the morning."

I nodded absently, chewing on my lip where my piercing had been. It itched like crazy. It was already closing up.

Mari glanced around, then reached out to give my knee a

squeeze. "We'll find him, Kat. I promise."

8

After my mom was killed, I went into a bit of a tailspin. It's a little embarrassing, really, but I was devastated, naïve, and pissed off—and in combination, those three things created a monster. I became a rash, unstable creature driven by a single thing: vengeance. It was my air and water and food. It was the blood pumping through my veins and the dreams disturbing my sleep. It was my everything.

And then Dom came in and gave me focus. He taught me discipline and how to fight. He gave me the skills and tools I needed to make vengeance a reality.

And then there was Nik, helping me understand the enemy. Helping me plan. Driving me ever onward and cautioning me when I exhibited too much recklessness. Until, one day, he pushed a few too many buttons, and I snapped. I almost died that day. On Mari's *anti-At* blade.

Maybe I'd still bear a closer resemblance to the Kat I used to be—the Kat who still had a mother and hopes for the future and a sparkle in her eye—if not for Dom and Nik and Mari. Maybe, but I also never would've avenged my mom. I didn't regret leaving the girl I used to be behind one bit. My heart was cold, my memory of the taste of vengeance crisp and clear. It had been delicious. Until it soured. Until those the Senate had me hunting no longer bore any resemblance to those responsible for my mother's death. Until it became bitter ash on my tongue.

But by then it was too late. By then, the girl I'd been was dead, a hard, empty shell left in her place.

Maybe that was why I felt such excitement about having seen Mari. She'd known me way back when. It was by Mari's side that I'd spent sixteen years hunting down those even remotely responsible for my mother's death. She'd seen the transformation. Hell, she'd been a part of the transformation. In a way, she reminded me of who I used to be. And I couldn't ignore the sense of grief I felt when thinking of that sad, lost girl.

I pulled my phone from my coat pocket as soon as I was out of the elevator and called the shop, figuring Nik was still lurking around. AKA covering for me. I was right. Kimi answered, but she retrieved Nik as soon as I asked for him. Good thing, because I didn't have his number, and I was going to explode if I didn't share what had just happened with someone.

"Hey, Kat—"

"You're *never* going to believe who I just saw," I told him.

"Who?" he asked. "And where are you? It's loud as fuck on your end."

"Oh . . ." I glanced around me, taking in the hustle and bustle of business professionals sneaking in an early lunch. There were so many of them, I doubted there were many people left up in their offices. "I'm in a food court," I told Nik. "Sorry. Hang on . . ." I weaved my way through the crowd of lunch-goers and made it to the glass doors to Fourth Avenue a good thirty seconds later.

I pushed through the rightmost door, only to be greeted by a blast of cold air and a crowd of people huddling on the covered stairs to stay out of the pouring rain. "Excuse me," I mumbled to one woman.

She shifted an inch. Unfortunately, I wasn't quite that thin. "Excuse me," I repeated.

A few glances were cast my way, but nobody really put any effort into moving.

So I did what any reasonable person would do—I raised my voice and broke out the big-kid words. "Oh for fuck's sake, *move*, people!"

I received shocked looks and grumbles from the crowd this time. But hey—they made a path that was just my size. What peaches.

I pulled up my hood and hunched my shoulders as I trudged up to the bus stop at the next block. I'd have taken my bike, but the outfit didn't really work on a motorcycle, especially not if I wanted to keep it looking nice. Not that *that* mattered now. My stupid "nice" boots had shitty traction on the wet cement, and I longed for my heavy-treaded combat boots.

"Sorry," I told Nik, again. I'd been holding the phone against my lapel when I'd shouted, but Nejeret ears were sensitive. "Anyway, I was at this open house thing at Ouroboros—that's the pharmaceutical company that—"

"I know who they are, Kat; I'm not a moron. Why were *you* there?"

I stopped walking, pressed my lips together, and inhaled and exhaled deeply. There was no reason for him to get all snippy with me just because I wasn't a slave to the idiot box like everybody else. "They're connected to all this somehow," I finally admitted.

Nik was quiet for a few seconds. "You knew they were connected to the disappearances and you went there anyway?"

My eyes bugged out. Sometimes he *was* a moron, whatever he said. "Why else would I go there?" I gave a derisive snort and continued up the hill. "It's not like *I* need to drink from the fountain of youth." Though a sip from the fountain of *un*-youth might do the trick. Especially if it would wrangle my pesky lingering teenage hormones. They could be a real bitch sometimes.

"Kat—"

"Mari was there," I said, flinging out the one thing that might waylay him from laying into me for being reckless, then held my breath.

"*What?*"

"Yeah, she's working for them. But really, she's undercover for the Senate. Did you know?"

"I didn't," he said. "But then, I haven't really been keeping up with things . . ."

"Right, well . . . that's crazy, right?" I reached the street corner at the top of the hill. "She's going to do some digging and see what she can find out about Dom. And—" I caught myself before I let it spill about the fishy shipment. I could check it out without him. No need to put anyone else in danger. Besides, I worked better on my own. Let's just say I have trust issues. I don't trust others not to do stupid shit and get themselves killed—like my mom—and I don't trust myself not to stop them.

"And *what?*" Nik asked.

"And . . . it was good to see her."

"Jesus, Kat." Disappointment was a loud, clear bell tolling in his voice.

"What?" I stopped some ways from the crowded bus stop and ducked under the ledge of another skyscraper.

"What the fuck were you thinking, going there alone—and without even letting me know?"

I reared back as though he'd slapped me. "Excuse me?" Since when was he my self-appointed keeper?

"They're the ones taking people—taking *us*—and you walked right into their house. They caught Dom, for fuck's sake. *Dom.* You think you're better than him? Really?"

"No, I just—"

"Then get your head out of your ass. A reckless move like that's what almost killed you last time." I shook my head as he spoke. How dare he? "This time, I might not be around to—"

"You know what," I cut in, voice raised. A few people turned their heads my way. I gave them the finger. "You can just fuck off, Nik. Just fuck the fuck off. Just walk away. Just disappear." I pulled the phone from my ear and stared at his name. "That's what you're best at," I said and hung up, fuming.

My phone started vibrating with an incoming call almost immediately. It was Nik. I rejected it. I did it twice more before I turned the damn thing on silent and stuffed it back into my pocket, grumbling "Asshole" under my breath.

I strolled into the East Precinct station with a chip on my shoulder and a bone to pick. I couldn't go back to the shop until I'd cooled off, but I also couldn't stand being unproductive. I marched straight to the unmanned reception window and dinged the little bell with equal parts purpose and ferocity. And just kept on dinging. It was their own damn fault for putting the thing out in the open in the first place.

Garth sprang up from behind his desk near the back of the room and hustled to the window, slamming his hand over mine to stop the dinging.

He looked at me and blinked several times, then his lips spread into an unsure grin. "I almost didn't recognize you like that."

I rolled my eyes. "Are you going to let me in, or what?" I

asked, gesturing to the locked door with my chin.

Garth released my hand and let me in. I followed him back to his desk.

"Gah . . ." I dragged a rolly chair over from the desk in front of his and plopped down. "I hate every single thing that I'm wearing."

"You look nice," Garth said, sitting at his desk and typing on his laptop. He clicked his mouse a few times, then settled back in his chair with his arms crossed over his broad chest. "So to what do I owe this visit?"

Resting my forearm across the corner of his desk, I leaned in and locked eyes with him. "Where are the files?" I sat back. "I can't do my part until you do yours . . ."

He frowned and reached for his mouse, pulling up a new window on his computer. "I sent them to you an hour ago." He looked at me. "You didn't get them?" He went back to scanning the screen. "The combined file size was pretty large, but it doesn't look like it bounced back."

I exhaled heavily and pulled my phone from my coat pocket. Sure enough, there was an email from the SPD. There was also a string of texts from Nik and one from Mari telling me the supposed location of her off-the-books shipment— Harbor Island. "No, no," I told Garth, pocketing my phone. "It's my fault. I just haven't checked my phone in a bit." I started combing my fingers through my hair, forgetting I'd pulled it back in a rare bun, and ended up pulling a few chunks free. "Damn it," I grumbled, taking down the whole thing.

"Everything alright?" Garth asked, a little wary.

"Yes," I snapped, then sighed. "No." I shook my head, laughing under my breath. *Damn you, Nik* . . . "Everything's really not alright." For whatever reason, he'd always been able to get under my skin, and his admonitions had cut pretty deep.

"Well . . ." Garth turned his wrist over to check his watch. "I had an early shift today. I was technically done thirty minutes ago, so if you want to head down to the Goose and grab a beer . . . ?"

I perked up. "Dear God, yes." I stood and looked down at him, still seated in his desk chair. "Are you ready?"

He chuckled. "Just give me a minute, alright?" He glanced over his shoulder. "Feel free to grab a coffee while you wait."

"No, I'm good."

"I think there might still be a few donuts back there, too."

I was already on my way.

Again, he chuckled. That deep, softly rumbling sound—and the fact that *I'd* caused it—eased my chip, just a bit.

As I took a bite of apple fritter, I realized something truly terrifying. I *liked* Garth. Like, he was a cool dude. He was interesting, and he cared about missing street kids—the kind most people considered pests and *wanted* to get rid of. He was a genuine good guy. And he was a fragile, short-lived human. A surefire path to heartbreak and devastation.

But I still wanted to grab a beer with him, despite knowing I shouldn't. Knowing I was asking for trouble. Nik was being an overprotective dick, I was sad and pissed, and Garth was being nice to me. It was a rare thing for me. A dangerous thing.

"Ready?" Garth asked, hand on my shoulder.

I jumped and turned around, half-eaten fritter to my chest.

"Sorry, didn't mean to scare you." He smiled, causing little crinkles at the corners of his coffee-brown eyes.

"S'okay," I said around a mouthful of donut.

He chuckled *again*, and I wanted to punch myself for thinking it was cute. I mean, this guy was at least ten years my junior. But then, I was getting to the age where hooking up with anyone my own age was pretty creepy, considering that *I* looked like I'd barely graduated from high school. It was getting harder and harder to shake the pedophile ick factor with anyone who didn't make me feel like Mrs. Robinson.

"You swear you're over twenty-one?" Garth asked me, eyes narrowed. "I don't want to get suspended for drinking with a minor using a fake ID."

I snorted, amused that his train of thought hadn't been far off from mine. "Trust me, bud. I'm good."

9

I drink too much. I know it, but it's hard to say no to the blissful numbness the bottle provides when I'm guaranteed to have zero side effects, at least health-wise. It's my favorite medicine, and for a good long while, it's been the only way I'm able to let my guard down enough to sleep with someone. Sometimes, it's the only way I can fall asleep. If only the dreams didn't kick in when the booze wore off. I'd probably smoke cigarettes, too, if they didn't make my hair smell like an ashtray and inspire me to spend half my day in the shower or brushing my teeth. Trust me, I'd tried.

"So," Garth said, watching me knock back my fourth shot of tequila, "bad day?" We'd been at the bar for maybe ten minutes. From the look on Garth's face, I was impressing the hell out of him with my gusto. Or was that shock? We'd grabbed street tacos from the food truck out front, and the Mexican food had inspired me to stick with a theme—tequila and Coronas. Oh yeah, did I mention I was sipping on a beer as well? Garth was being a smart human and sticking to beer alone.

I laughed bitterly, then took a bite of one of my tacos—shredded pork belly with cilantro-lime slaw, hot-hot salsa, and extra guac. Better than a frozen pizza, that's for damn sure. "I'd tell you just how bad," I said after swallowing. I glanced at him sidelong. "But then I'd have to kill you."

Garth laughed.

I eyed him as I took another bite. He thought I was joking. That's adorable.

"I'm going to hit the head," Garth said, standing from his stool. "Be right back."

As he made his way to the back of the room, I caught the bartender's eye at the far end of the bar—it was a different one from the chick who'd been serving us—and pointed to my empty shot glass. I watched him refill it, grabbing the bottle before he could take it away. "Just leave it," I said, looking into his Caribbean-blue eyes. His *Nejeret* eyes.

Not even an ounce of shock shone on his ageless face. A handsome face, even with that cruel twist to his mouth and the challenge glinting in his aqua eyes. Or maybe *because* of those things. Regardless, it was an unfamiliar face as well. This Nejeret wasn't part of Clan Heru.

"I haven't seen you around before." My lips spread into a slow grin. "Does Heru know you're working in his territory?"

He released the bottle but didn't answer.

"Do you know who I am?"

With a blink, he was looking at me again. He nodded. "Rogue Hunter." It had been my title back when I'd been working as one of the Senate's pet assassins, chowing down on revenge with a side of hefty paycheck.

My smile widened to a grin. "Does Heru know you're here?" I repeated. "Show me your papers." Though the Senate's way of tracking and regulating Nejerets was easily forgeable, at least it would give me this one's name. Of course, even if he had residency papers granting him permission to work and live here, there was no way for me to verify their authenticity without calling up Heru himself. And *that* wasn't going to happen. I was out. Done. He was still involved in Senate shit, and I wanted no part of that.

Besides, they were all better off without me.

"Don't have any," the bartending Nejeret said.

My eyes narrowed.

"Don't need them. I work for the Senate."

I scoffed. "Why would they station anyone on Cap Hill? I'm the only one who lives—" My eyes widened, and my lips parted as realization struck. He was here to keep an eye on me, the wild card. The loose cannon. The ex-assassin with too much time on her hands.

That cruel twist to his mouth broadened to a sly grin, and damn my neglected libido to hell if I wasn't equal parts turned on and pissed. How long had he been spying on me? And why? Just to make sure I didn't turn on the Senate themselves? Did he know I was investigating Ouroboros? Or the missing Nejerets? What about the street kids? Did he know that Nik was in town, staying with me? Nik hadn't wanted the Senate to know either of us were involved in the case—because he didn't trust that they weren't involved on the other end.

What if Nik was right? What would that mean for Mari? What if the Senators who'd sent her to Ouroboros were really involved in some sort of a hidden faction—a shadow Senate?

My blood chilled as I continued to stare into the Nejeret's eyes. Without warning, he plucked the bottle from my loose grip and replaced it on the counter behind him, swapping it out for a two-thirds-full bottle of Grand Centenario from the second-to-top shelf. He set the new bottle on the bar, met my eyes, and said, "On the house."

I uncorked the bottle, filled two shot glasses, and offered one to him, my not-so-sneaky way of checking if he'd spiked it with something. He clinked his glass against mine and tossed back the shot. I did the same. "Don't think this gets me off your back," I said, throat burning. I took a swig of my beer. "We *will* have a little chat. I want answers." I flicked the bottle with a fingernail. "But this'll buy you an hour or two."

He picked up my empty shot glasses, leaving only one behind, locked eyes with me, and licked his lips, that wicked grin returning. "I look forward to it."

My belly gave a little tingly flutter, and I crossed my legs on the stool. Now I was looking forward to our chat, too, and not for the words that would be exchanged. I cleared my throat, averted my gaze, and nodded to Garth, who was just returning from the bathroom. "Grab my friend another beer." As an afterthought, I added, "Please."

"You got it," the Nejeret bartender said and turned to fill a pint glass at the tap. He set it on the counter, then retreated to the other end of the bar.

"So . . ." Garth sat and took a swig of beer, draining his first pint glass and sliding it out of the way. "What was that all about?"

I held my finger up to my lips. "Shhh . . ." Reaching for the tequila bottle, I leaned closer to Garth and whispered. "He's got really good hearing, you know, because he's like me." I filled the shot glass, emptied it, and filled it again, then met Garth's dubious gaze. "A *witch*."

His eyes didn't widen, and he didn't laugh. Instead, he leaned in a little and spoke so quietly that I wouldn't have been able to hear him over the classic rock blaring throughout the bar without my Nejeret senses. "I know what you are . . . Nejeret."

Shit. Balls. If he shared even that name with the wrong person—if the wrong person overheard him and reported it to the Senate—they wouldn't hesitate in issuing a kill order, and whoever had taken my and Mari's places would hunt down Garth and silence him, for good.

"I have to go," I said, hopping off my barstool. I couldn't ever see him again; it would only put him in danger. I slapped a wad of cash on the bar and made a beeline for the door.

Garth's hand closed around my arm. "Kat, wait . . ."

I twisted my arm, yanking it free. "Stay away from me, Garth, and keep that word to yourself. Trust me, it's better for your health," I said, before turning and stalking out of the bar.

10

"Hey! Ink Witch!"

I stopped in my tracks, barely a dozen steps out of the bar, and spun around to glare at the Nejeret bartender. "What?" I snapped. I *really* hated that nickname.

The Nejeret's wicked grin was back, as was the challenging glint in his cerulean eyes. "What about our chat?" he said as he strode my way.

Frustrated and irritated after that little scene with Garth, I turned and continued down the sidewalk.

His quick footsteps told me he was jogging to catch up. He planted his hand on the brick wall in front of me just before the corner of the building, intending to block my retreat, but I ducked under his arm, barely missing a step. His next move was to grab my arm, just as Garth had, and pull me a few steps into the alley between the bar and the salon in the next building over.

I froze, giving his hand a pointed look, then raising my gaze to meet his. "I'm not in the mood to chat anymore."

He stepped closer and stared down at me, interest lighting his eyes. "Then what *are* you in the mood for?"

With the adrenaline pumping through my veins, making my heart race and exaggerating the rise and fall of my chest, I was itching for a fight. Or a fuck. Either would do. I stood on tiptoes and brought my lips nearer to his ear. "I don't think you can handle what I'm in the mood for." I dropped my heels, locking eyes with his.

The corner of his mouth lifted, exaggerating that cruel twist to his lips. "Try me."

I tilted up my chin just a fraction of an inch, and in the next heartbeat, his lips were on mine and my back was against the brick wall. His lips were soft, but his tongue was greedy and his rough stubble scratched my face. He tasted like tequila, mint, and just a hint of cigarettes. There was nothing gentle about him or his kiss—it was rough, cruel, and just a little painful when he bit my lip. It was exactly what I'd needed.

One of his hands tangled in my loose hair, yanking my head back even as he deepened the kiss. His other hand glided up my rib cage under my shirt, shoving my bra up and out of the way. He palmed my right breast, pinching the nipple between two fingers. When he twisted it just a tad too far, I arched my back and whimpered from the intoxicating mixture of pleasure and pain.

His leg slipped between mine, and my hips rocked against him, creating a blissful friction.

Someone gasped, a kid giggled, and a woman said, "Disgusting!"

The bartender—I still didn't know his name—broke the kiss, leaving me breathless and blocking my view of the alley mouth and whoever we'd disturbed with our little show. "I'm renting a place upstairs," he said into my hair. "Want to—"

I nodded.

He grabbed my hand and practically dragged me to a metal door further down the alleyway. He fished a key out of his pocket and unlocked the door, then pulled me in through the doorway to a dingy stairwell that smelled faintly of mildew. We never made it any further than that.

He unbuttoned my jeans and yanked them down without bothering with the zipper, then spun me around and, hands on my wrists, placed my palms on the smudged wall. His fingers slipped into the front of my underwear, and I dropped my head as he deftly found my most sensitive place. Damn, but this was exactly what I needed. No frills. No strings. No emotions. I craved a momentary reprieve from the insanity dragging me back into a world I'd extricated myself from years ago.

I could hear the clink-clink of metal on metal, then the sound of a zipper. A second later, the bartender pushed down my underwear, his other hand moving from between my legs to curl around the front of my neck, and the hard length of him slid between my thighs. He kicked my feet apart, spreading my legs as wide as my jeans would allow, and I arched my back, offering him a better angle. It did the trick. He slid into me in one rough motion.

"Oh fuck," he breathed.

I gasped at the pressure, at the relief, and rested my forehead against the wall.

"Do you know what it's like?" he asked, pulling out and slamming back into me. "Watching you on the nights you go home with someone?"

"Pervert," I said, grunting when he moved his hips in that jerky motion again. A slow burn thrummed to life in my belly, stoking hotter with each of his thrusts.

He leaned into me, pressing his chest against my back and curling his arm around my middle. His hand dipped lower, and I gasped when he pinched that swollen bundle of nerve endings. "I wondered . . . what it would feel like . . . to be them . . . to be inside you . . . fucking you."

"Well now"—an inferno roared low in my belly, seeking a

way out—"you know." I ground against his fingers as the pressure built to blissful heights within me.

"You're a little whore . . . aren't you?" His breath was hot against my cheek. "A dangerous little whore."

I squeezed my eyes shut, trying to block out his words even as I reached for sweet release.

His fingers stilled, and his thrusting slowed.

"No," I whispered. I was so close. So very close.

"Open your eyes, Kat," he said. "Look at me. Look at me and tell me you're a little whore, and I'll let you come."

I gritted my teeth, reaching for that glittering bliss, but he knew exactly what he was doing. He moved just slow enough to keep me on the edge—to hold me on the cusp of orgasm without letting me topple over the edge.

"Look at me, Kat. Tell me what you are."

I opened my eyes and glared at him. I was desperate for that moment of ecstasy. But my pride was non-negotiable. "Fuck you."

"I think you're already doing that, sweetheart." His breath was hot and sticky against my cheek, and I wanted nothing more than to have his hands off me. His mouth away from me. His dick anywhere but where it was right now.

"Not anymore," I said a moment before I jerked my head back, enjoying the crunch of his nose smashing against the back of my skull. It was almost as satisfying as sexual release. Almost, and maybe just a little bit more.

His hands flew to his face and I yanked up my jeans as I spun around, kneeing him in the groin, then raising my boot to kick him against the other side of the stairwell. "Fucking bitch," he said through a groan, blood seeping down his chin beneath his hands.

"Maybe," I said, pushing the stairwell door open. I stood

in the doorway and glared at him. "But I'm nobody's whore." I walked out into the alleyway, donkey-kicking the door shut behind me. Guess it was a fight I was looking for after all.

I jogged the five blocks to my shop, disgust and regret a lump of lead in my stomach. I never should've let that shithead Senate Nejeret put his hands on me in the first place. I slowed to a walk when my boot touched my native curb. I couldn't wait to get out of my clothes and back into something normal. Something clean. Something that didn't smell like *him*.

I pulled the shop door open and paused six steps in to glare at the man working in my office. Nik was leaning over a woman getting her tramp stamp covered up. I rushed past the door, not wanting to give him a chance to take in my all-too-recognizable scent. With his sensitive nose, there was no way he'd miss the smell of sex if I lingered.

The door's little bell chimed, and I glanced over my shoulder. "Oh, you've got to be kidding me," I said under my breath as Garth strode in. I stalked toward him. "What did I just tell you?" I said, seething. I really didn't want to get him killed, and that was exactly what would happen if the wrong Nejeret discovered that he, a lowly human, knew about us. Protecting ourselves, our people, was our number-one priority. We might be more powerful and live longer than humans, but they outnumbered us a million to one. Probably more. "Stay away from me, Garth."

His eyes shifted to the right, then to the left. Kimi was watching us from behind the counter, but the artists and clients in the offices seemed oblivious enough. Except for Nik, I'm sure. He was probably soaking up every single word. "I still need your help with the missing kids . . ."

Nope. Not happening. With his knowledge, if I got him involved with this Ouroboros situation and the missing Nejerets . . . his days were numbered, probably in the single digits. I shook my head and rolled my eyes, putting on an air of annoyance, which wasn't all that difficult. "Fine, whatever." My mind churned a mile a minute. "Meet me at the Fremont Troll at nine, tonight." Waiting for me there would keep him distracted while I searched the containers in Mari's mysterious shipment. "You can help me go through the missing kids' shit."

His brows knitted together. "Why not now?"

Because I need to know that you're somewhere else when I go to Harbor Island. "I have to prep some stuff," I told him, which wasn't exactly a lie. "Ask the cards for guidance . . ."

His eyes scrutinized my face, but finally, he nodded. "Alright. Nine o'clock tonight—the troll."

I nodded, then turned away from him and strode toward the beaded curtain, glancing sidelong at Nik as I passed by.

He was studiously not looking at me. Until his nostrils flared and his entire body stiffened. His jaw tensed, but he remained focused on his client. *My* client. There was no doubt in my mind that he'd been eavesdropping, but at the moment I was more concerned with what his nose was picking up than what his ears had.

I paused before the beaded curtain, like I might offer an explanation or an excuse. But there were none that didn't make me sound like the degenerate I'd become. So I continued on. I passed through the curtain, shame bubbling in my belly and disgust poisoning my heart. Because Nik knew. And if I wasn't mistaken by his reaction, he *cared.*

Even more disturbing—so did I. And that scared the shit out of me.

11

I emerged from the shower with skin raw and rosy from excessive scrubbing. By the time I was lacing up my combat boots, my head was clear of the slosh and slog of too much tequila and my regrettable sexual encounter. I still didn't know the Senate Nejeret's name, but it didn't change the fact that I felt immeasurably better once the scent of him was off my body and I was comfy in my favorite pair of jeans and a tank top. Though it was the boots that really sealed the deal. Feeling like me again made everything else that was going wrong seem a little less vomit-worthy.

I grabbed a leftover slice of pizza from the fridge and headed into my office. The paint on the walls had changed again, becoming a dark, swirling miasma. I studied the designs, searching for meaning in the chaos while I ate the cold pizza. The only definite shape I could make out was a pitch-black orb that seemed to bob along throughout the midnight current.

Maybe, eventually it would make sense, but right now it was meaningless to me. I brushed the crumbs on my fingers off on my jeans and walked to the closet. I stared at the door for a solid minute. Was I really going to do this? After three full years of relative normalcy, was I really considering jumping back into this life—one where I needed a sword at my back and a half-dozen other blades stowed about my person? Once I opened this door, once I came face-to-face with the darkness within—with my past—I wasn't sure I'd be able to shut it away again.

But for Dom . . .

To find him, to save him, I needed the darkness. Wasn't that why Nik had come to me in the first place? Not only because my *sheut* might make me the only one who could find him, but because I, personally, might be the only one willing to do what needs to be done to save him.

"You better not already be dead," I grumbled, sliding the closet door open and ignoring the lead sinking into the pit of my stomach.

The closet was empty, for the most part. Two identical small wood and iron chests sat on the closet floor, and a few items hung on hangers. I dragged the chests out into the room, then reached up to the overhead shelf, fingers searching for the only thing up there. For a moment, I thought it wasn't there. My heart skipped a few beats. But my fingertips grazed a strip of leather, then touched cold metal, and my worry eased.

I closed my hand around the old, familiar hilt of my sword, Mercy, and pulled it down from the shelf. "Hello, old friend," I murmured. I'd named the sword a long time ago, and it seemed wrong to ignore what she'd been to me. She was what had finally brought an end to the suffering left over from my human life. She was my right hand. My salvation.

Overall, Mercy was very katana-like. Her blade was long, slender, and slightly curved, with only one sharp edge, and the hilt was wrapped in worn black leather cording, leaving the shiny steel underneath peeking through in a diamond pattern. The butt of the hilt was solid silver, a Horus falcon molded into the metal, tarnished from the years of disuse. But however much it seemed like a katana, this sword was different. Mercy was ancient beyond any katana, and so very *other*. She'd been created by Nik, her *At* blade formed by his hands nearly two thousand years ago.

I unsheathed Mercy in one slow, smooth motion. The sound of her indestructible, crystalline *At* blade sliding against steel broke a dam in my mind, and memories flooded in. So many memories. So many lives. So many names crossed off a list with the slice of this blade through flesh and bone. My heart rate increased as adrenaline spiked my blood. I was ready. To fight. To kill. And if it came down to it, to avenge.

"Soon," I said to the bloodthirsty creature I'd just reawakened within me. Depending on what I found at Harbor Island, it could be *very* soon. I sheathed the sword. Soon, but not yet.

Kneeling, I set Mercy on the floor and opened the first of the chests. It had been so long since I'd stowed them in the closet, I couldn't remember which was which. One contained my stash of weapons and gear, the other, what would probably convince a criminal profiler that I was a serial killer. To some, maybe I was. But I hadn't killed for pleasure or for the thrill, even if, for a time, it had provided temporary relief from the grief. I'd killed with purpose. I'd killed for a cause. My cause, and the Senate's.

As soon as I lifted the lid, I closed my eyes and bowed my head. This chest didn't contain any weapons. Instead, it was filled with mementos—reminders—of the thirty-nine lives I'd taken during Mari's and my sanctioned reign of terror. As the Senate's assassins hunting rogues, rebel Nejerets, we'd taken out fifty-one targets total. I'd finished off most, not because I enjoyed taking lives, but because I enjoyed watching Mari torment our targets—our victims—less. We'd both lost our mothers to those rogues, and the hunger for vengeance could twist even the purest soul into a monster willing to do unthinkable things in the quest to sate the insatiable.

I opened my eyes and made myself peer into the chest. I reached in and pulled out the first thing my gaze landed on— a small, black leather-bound notebook. It had belonged to a Nejeret named Gerald, the last Nejeret I ever killed for the Senate. The last life I took. He'd been a deserter, running for his life, but he hadn't been a true rogue—the proof was in that little black book—and he'd been the furthest thing from dangerous. He'd been terrified. He'd begged me not to kill him. He'd cried, in the end, when I'd freed his *ba* with one slice of Mercy's ever-sharp blade.

Groping blindly behind me, I found my sketch pad and the pen I'd left in here last time, among the droves of sketches of the missing Nejerets. I wrote down Gerald's first and last name. My victim's name. Sure, his *ba*—his everlasting soul— was out there, somewhere, maybe on this plane, maybe another, but his physical life had been ended by me. That mattered. I'd killed, and as with all the others, I'd also killed a part of me. Taking his life had been a breaking point for me, tipping me over the edge. The moment his heart stopped, I knew I was done. I'd felt it deep in my bones.

It was past time I acknowledged all that I'd done. It was time for me to accept it—finally—and, if I could, move on.

I pulled the next item out of the chest. A flyer advertising an animal adoption fair. It had been stuck to Bree Coolridge's fridge. She'd been hiding from us for six years and had amassed a small army of rescue animals. She'd had no less than seven cats, three dogs, and a turtle when Mari and I finally tracked her down. She'd been instrumental in orchestrating the events that led up to my mother's murder. I hadn't felt an ounce of pity for her when my blade pierced her heart, but I had felt bad for her animals. I hoped they found new homes afterward.

I added Bree's name below Gerald's, the act cathartic.

I moved through the chest, cataloguing and recording names until I had a list of thirty-nine. I tore the page free from my sketch pad and folded it up, tucking it into my back pocket, then returned everything to the chest and shut it once more. I shoved the chest back into the closet, vowing to never open it again. The next time I pulled it out would be to destroy it and everything within. I would honor my victims another way from now on.

Going through the second chest was a far less draining experience. I gathered the items I needed—two knives and their matching boot sheaths, a bracelet that doubled as a garrote, two four-inch needle daggers, and a leather belt that concealed a stubby push dagger in the buckle. I set everything on the floor beside me and returned that chest to the closet as well.

Once the closet doors were closed, I pushed everything to the side of the room, clearing a large space. I drew the sword and set the sheath and shoulder harness on the floor by the wall with the rest of my gear. It had been years since I'd wielded Mercy, and though I kept in fighting shape, I was out of practice with a weapon.

I spent the next few hours reconnecting with my sword. Her balance, the way she cut through the air, the way she worked as an extension of me—it all felt both familiar and foreign at the same time. I practiced with Mercy, spinning, thrusting, parrying, and rolling, until only familiarity remained.

When I emerged from my office, sweaty but oddly energized, the oven clock said it was five in the afternoon. I was planning to leave for the shipyard at eight. I had three more hours to kill.

I pulled a frozen pizza—BBQ chicken—from the freezer and turned on the oven. Too hungry to wait a half hour for the pie to be done, I peeked into the cupboard to the right of the stove, fingers crossed that it wouldn't be empty.

"Score," I sang quietly, pulling down an unopened bag of Hot Cheetos. They're terrible for me, I know, but that knowledge never stops me from inhaling a whole bag in a single sitting. And I'm not talking about one of the little bags. Think: family size. I tore the Cheetos open and shoved a handful into my mouth, then grabbed a Cherry Coke from the fridge. Leaning back against the counter, I alternated between scarfing down Cheetos and swigging Coke. I wholeheartedly accept that I'm the poster child for what not to eat. But then, I'm the poster child for what not to *fill-in-the-blank*, so why hold back?

I chomped on a few Cheetos.

How to kill the time?

I drank from the can of Coke. I ate a few more Cheetos. I looked around the fairly barren apartment, utterly uninspired.

An idea tiptoed into my mind, and I tilted my head from side to side, considering it. I set the pop can down on the counter behind me and pulled the list of names from my back pocket. I unfolded the paper, reading over the list as I sucked the spicy fake-cheese dust from my fingertips, scraping the stubbornest bits with my teeth.

I checked the clock on the stove. The oven was almost heated, and I was down to two hours and fifty-four minutes. I had a tattoo in mind for my left forearm, a piece to replace the fading tarot card, and I'd been playing with the idea of something else that would test the extent of my innate *sheut* power. I'd be cutting it close, time-wise, but if I wasn't done by the time I had to leave, I could always finish inking myself later.

The oven beeped, and I tossed the pizza on the rack, setting the timer before I headed for the door to the stairs. The shop closed early on Sundays, so there was a good chance that everybody had already left. Kimi might still be here, closing out the register and doing the final clean-up, but everyone else *should* be gone for the day. I crossed my fingers. Hopefully that included Nik. The idea of facing him right now, after everything that happened earlier . . . I couldn't handle it.

Thankfully, everyone, Kimi included, was gone. Even Nik. I didn't know where he'd gone or for how long, and at the moment, I didn't really care. I *didn't*. The shop was empty, and I was alone. Which was exactly what I'd been hoping for.

I paused at the beaded curtain.

So why was disappointment taking root in my chest?

Hands in fists and nails digging into my palms, I ignored the troublesome emotion and pushed through the curtain. I gathered up my tattoo machine, a fresh needle, and a bottle of black ink, then paused, staring into the ink drawer. Tucked in the very back was a bottle that almost seemed to be glowing, ethereal and iridescent.

I grinned, swapping out the black ink for Nik's *At* ink, and retreated back upstairs.

I stared at my left palm wondering what exactly I'd just created. A shimmery Eye of Horus stared back at me, taking up nearly my entire palm, reflecting colors from another dimension every time I shifted my hand and the light hit my skin differently. It was my clan's symbol, proclaiming my permanent obedience to Heru better than any papers or oath ever could. But it was more than that, too.

The Eye of Horus was an ancient symbol, steeped with so much meaning—thousands of years' worth. A civilization's worth. An entire mythology's worth. It was a symbol of protection from evil, from deceivers . . . from so many things. I didn't know how it would work, or if it would even do anything beyond being decorative, but I figured a symbol as potent as the Eye of Horus would have as good of a chance as anything of doing *something*. And gods knew I could use some protection right about now.

Learning how to use the powers afforded me by my *sheut* was a game of trial and error. I never really knew what would work and what wouldn't. I'd barely had the damn thing for three years. It had been a gift from the two new true gods—the Netjer, the inheritors of our universe—who'd been born just twenty years ago to Lex and Heru. And—laugh—*I* was their aunt. On the same day they'd gifted me my *sheut*, they'd left our universe and had yet to return. Sometimes it felt like they never would.

I closed my fist, then opened it again, somewhat surprised I couldn't feel the tattoo. It had healed almost as soon as I'd inked it, as usual, but I still thought I should be able to feel a stiffness or *something*. The depiction of the goddess Isis in *At* ink on my right arm had been the same way. It just looked like something that I should feel. But I didn't.

I glanced at the clock. Six-thirty. An hour and a half until it was go-time.

Cracking my neck, I re-inked the needle in the bottle of shimmering, liquid *At* and looked at the sheet of paper listing the names of everyone I'd killed. It was time to get to work on my next piece, on my memorial to every life I'd ended . . . and to every piece of myself I'd killed along the way. I brought the needle to my wrist and pressed it against my skin, starting with a *G*.

12

The rumble of the Ducati echoed off buildings as I rode through downtown Seattle. As usual, an accident had jammed up I-5, turning the southbound lanes into a glorified parking lot. It wasn't a major loss; I'd only have been on the freeway for a couple miles anyway, and this way I didn't have to deal with the high stress of lane-splitting. I was already anxious enough.

Garth would realize I'd sent him on a wild goose chase soon enough, but at least this would keep him from being able to follow me. And just maybe, after getting stood up tonight, he'd get the hint; our partnership was over. And then there was Nik. I didn't know where he'd gone after filling in for me at the shop today, but I had a pretty damn good guess. I'd eat my boots if he wasn't heading to the Fremont Troll to spy on me. After all, he'd overheard my exchange with Garth. I hoped my instincts were correct. I wanted both of them as far away from this Ouroboros mess as possible. I was expendable; they weren't.

Is it weird that I was also a little giddy? It had been ages—*years*—since I'd seen any real action. The violent kind, not the sexy kind. My little scuffle with Nik two nights back had awakened something within me, almost like him showing up had started a domino effect that would drag me back into this world, kicking and screaming, if need be. Except I was going willingly.

I zigzagged through the streets of SoDo, the Industrial District south of downtown Seattle, and parked my bike on the east side of the Spokane Street Bridge, not wanting to alert whatever late-night workers or security personnel were lingering around on Harbor Island of my presence. Kickstand lowered, I hopped off the bike and hung my helmet on the upraised handlebar, then jogged to the West Seattle Bridge Trail, which crossed the Duwamish Waterway and carried pedestrians and bicyclists across man-made Harbor Island at ground level. It was dark out and cold at just past nine at night—nobody was on the trail.

Harbor Island was a funny place—I'd been here once on a field trip for my high school economics class. We were supposed to see international commerce at work on the enormous man-made island, but we really just ended up watching an hour-long safety movie about container ships and shipyard hazards, listening to a rep from the company that runs Terminal 18—the shipping container facility taking up the northeast quadrant of Harbor Island—explain pretty much everything there was to know about containers. It was disappointing, especially since many of us had been fantasizing about climbing all over the neat stacks of thousands of containers we were only allowed to view through a razor wire–topped chain-link fence.

I reached said chain-link fence, specifically the portion blocking off the south side of the industrial part of Harbor Island, and drew my sword. One of my favorite things about Mercy was that her *At* blade could cut through pretty much anything, and the wire making up a chain-link fence was about as resistant to my sword as chilled butter to a table knife; cutting through wasn't effortless, but it didn't make me sweat, either. Within five minutes, I'd cut an opening about four feet high—tall enough for me to squeeze through without resorting to crawling.

I'd taken three cautious steps onto the parking lot of Harley Marine Services when a motion-activated floodlight winked on.

"Shit," I hissed, slinking another dozen steps to crouch between two large white service trucks. I waited for a minute or two, listening for footsteps and engines. Hearing none, I straightened a little and made my way across the lot, moving in the shadows between vehicles whenever possible.

The next lot had to belong to an auto shipping company, because it basically looked like the lot of a car dealership. And a damn fancy one. It worked perfectly for my purposes. I managed to cross to the north end of the lot without tripping any more motion sensors.

After that, the east half of the man-made island was all Terminal 18. I stood at the edge of the packed car lot between two sedans, their black paint gleaming like oil in the dim moonlight. There was a fairly large open stretch of asphalt before the never-ending rows of red, blue, green, and orange shipping containers started, some stacked four or five high. On the far right, following the island's artificial shoreline, clusters of cranes in twos and threes stood sentinel, burnt-orange behemoths watching over everything.

I snuck to the water's edge, hoping any motion sensors for floodlights or cameras wouldn't reach that far since the movement of the water would be constantly setting them off. Keeping low and moving slowly, I made my way further into Terminal 18.

Mari's text from that morning had mentioned that the

Ouroboros containers belonging to the illicit shipment would be stored between slots A-27 and A-30. According to the satellite maps I'd scoured online, row A was nearest to the water. Meaning it should be just straight ahead.

I squinted as I neared the first stack of containers—a stack of two, both green and both painted with the John Deere logo on the side. They were in spot A-13. The next stack, three containers in spot A-17—two orange, one red—were unlabeled, so far as I could see, besides a series of nonsensical numbers and letters on the door side.

I scanned the white numbers painted on the asphalt ahead. Sure enough, ten spots down, I found A-27. A stack of three containers piled one atop the other, all blue, called me onward, followed immediately by a stack of four. I jogged ahead, heart pounding and blood a raging river in my ears.

"Alright, you shitstains," I said under my breath as I reached the supposed Ouroboros containers. "What are you hiding?" I stopped beside the stack of three, surveilling the long sides facing me. There was nothing to identify them as actually belonging to Ouroboros, so I moved around to the water side, where the container's doors might give me some hint that I was in the right spot.

They didn't—like so many of the containers filling the yard, they were labeled only with a series of letters and numbers, none of which made sense to me.

I took a step backward, peering at all four stacks of solid blue containers. I placed my hands on my hips and chewed on my bottom lip. They were right where Mari had said they would be, but there was only one way to find out if these were the right containers—the same way I would find out what the hell Ouroboros was up to. I had to break into them.

Drawing my sword slowly enough that the ring of *At* on

steel was minimal, I approached the first stack. The lock on the bottom container looked complex and heavy duty, and there was no way for me to tell whether or not it was rigged with some kind of an alarm. But who says I have to go through the lock to get into the container? It would take some time and a fair amount of elbow grease, but Mercy was more than capable of cutting through the thick sheet of steel.

The tip of my sword was inches from the container's door when I heard the creak of metal on metal. I froze, sword gripped in both hands and breath held, and scanned the containers around me.

The door of the second container in a stack of five in slot A-30 inched open.

I pulled back Mercy and raised my elbows, settling into a ready stance.

Something tumbled out of the container, falling at least eight feet to the pavement. It landed with an oomph and a groan. Not a some*thing*, a some*one*.

"Kat? Is that you?" It was Mari—the someone. She pushed herself off the ground a few inches and raised her head. There was barely a crescent of a moon high overhead, and across the water, Seattle far outshone the stars, but my eyes were good enough to see the lab coat she was wearing. And the bloodstains marring the fabric and the dark bruises on her face and neck. She looked like hell beaten over.

My palm itched, and I rubbed it against my jeans. "What the hell are you doing here, Mars?"

Mari coughed a laugh, spitting up something that looked suspiciously like blood. "Your concern is underwhelming, as usual."

Hesitantly, I sheathed my sword and approached, offering her a hand up. Someone must've caught her poking around, but that didn't explain how she'd ended up *in* one of the containers she'd all but sent me here to find.

She accepted my outstretched hand, pulling herself up to a sitting position but not even attempting to stand. She coughed weakly and clutched one side like the action hurt her ribs. "I need a minute . . ."

I nodded, still rubbing my palm against my jeans. "Is anything broken?" Because if she had any broken bones, I had no doubt she'd prefer for me to set them now rather than wait until they'd healed so much that they'd have to be re-broken to heal properly.

She shook her head, her dark bob matted in chunks. "Not for me. I don't know about Dom . . ."

"What do you mean—Dom?" I scanned the area, searching for his lanky form but finding no sign of him. "Is he here? Where? What happened?"

"We snuck out together." She pointed up to the partially open container with her chin. "He's up there. He's in pretty bad shape, though."

Before she'd finished speaking, I'd launched myself at the container, grabbing hold of the lip. My feet scrabbled for purchase on the vertically ribbed face of the bottom container. The toe of my boot found the boxed lock, and I used that to leverage myself the rest of the way up.

It was even darker inside the container, the sliver of light spilling in through the opening barely enough to allow even my heightened Nejeret vision to make out the interior.

But I could see Dom, lying on the floor a couple yards in. Pallets laden with boxes filled the space beyond him, their shrink-wrap gleaming dully in the barely there light.

"Dom," I said, rushing forward and dropping to my knees beside him. I turned his head so I could see his face. "Dom, are you alright?"

No response.

My heart turned to lead.

I pressed my fingers to his neck in search of a pulse, letting out a relieved breath when I found it, faint but steady enough for now. So long as his heart was beating, propelling his Nejeret blood through his body, and so long as his injuries weren't immediately fatal, he'd be able to regenerate.

I shook him by the shoulder. "Dom, can you hear me?"

But still, he said nothing. He did nothing. He was out cold. But I could see him; I could touch him. It was a far cry from the position I'd been in an hour ago, and I couldn't ignore the burst of euphoria that sprouted in my chest. The hard part was over. I'd found him. It would all be downhill from here.

13

The first time I met Mari, she almost killed me. In her defense, I was trying to kill her. She's the opposite of Nik, able to pull a far more dangerous and volatile universal energy into this realm, give it form, and shape it to her will. It was with that energy that she nearly killed not only my body, but also my eternal soul.

The universe was created by the old gods, Re and Apep, around a principle of absolute, ultimate balance known as *ma'at*. If *At* is the principle element of creation, then *anti-At* is its inverse—destruction. It binds to *At*, binds to every aspect of creation, moving it, changing it, keeping the universe from growing stagnant. We are, all of us, objects of creation, of *At*. Nejerets carry a little piece of *At* within us, in the form of our *ba*—our soul. Should we come into physical contact with *anti-At*, we'll change. The *anti-At* particles, torn from their usual plane of existence, become ravenous in their need to destroy, binding with anything and everything. Binding with us, consuming our *ba*, until we no longer exist. Until we *never* existed at all. If we come into contact with anti-At, we'll be *unmade*.

Which is precisely what almost happened to me, a long time ago, when Mari nearly killed me. Nik and I had fought, much like this morning, and I'd run off, dead set on avenging my mother's death. I'd attacked Mari, mistakenly believing she was responsible, and she'd stabbed me. With a gleaming black dagger made of pure *anti-At*. Only Nik arriving seconds later and extracting all of the otherworldly poison from my body by binding every molecule of *anti-At* with its one true mate, *At*, had allowed me to survive. Not unscathed—my *ba* had been damaged and would forever bear the scars—but I hadn't been unmade, either.

Mari had gone from my enemy to my ally in a matter of minutes. We'd been through hell together, and she was like a sister to me, even if we hadn't spoken in years. There weren't many people I'd trust with my life, but if push came to shove, I'd trust Mari.

"Mars," I called through the container door. "Can you give me a hand?" I dragged Dom to the door by his armpits. "We need to get him out of here." He wasn't wearing anything substantial, just a pair of sweatpants and a white T-shirt—both torn and covered with bloodstains that looked black in the dim light—and he felt far too cold for my liking.

"I'm still too weak," Mari said from outside. "I'll just end up dropping him. Where's Nik? He could help you."

I frowned, my hand burning. "He's not here." I set Dom down a half-dozen inches from the edge and poked my head out through the opening. "How long until you're strong enough? We need to get him out of here before anyone notices we're here." A thought struck me, and I realized we might be under a far greater time crunch than I'd previously thought. "Do they know this is how you escaped? Will they come looking for you here?"

Mari was still sitting on the ground, legs folded beneath her, back hunched, and hands in her lap. She shook her head. "I should be mostly recovered in fifteen minutes or so. They worked me over pretty good. Do you have anything to eat? That'd speed it up . . ."

I reached into the right zippered pocket of my leather jacket and pulled out the protein bar I'd stashed there before leaving my apartment. Never leave home without one. "What happened, anyway?" I asked, tossing the bar to Mari.

She tore into the wrapper with gusto. "They caught me nosing around in a restricted lab over there," she said, nodding back toward the rest of SoDo sprawling behind her. "I found the missing Nejerets, but I was only able to get Dom out. He didn't look too hot when I found him, but he was still able to help me fight our way out." She stuffed the last piece of the protein bar into her mouth, balled up the wrapper, and threw it on the ground a few feet away. "We should find Nik and go back for the others."

I glanced down at my palm. It burned something fierce now, like I held a handful of stinging nettles. My eyebrows drew together. Despite the very real and very uncomfortable sensation, there didn't seem to be anything wrong with the skin of my palm. It wasn't red or swollen, and the Eye of Horus looked the same, gleaming in the subdued evening light.

"Where is Nik, anyway?" Mari asked. "I thought he'd be with you."

"Don't know," I said, shrugging. "Don't care." Why was she obsessing about him all of a sudden? They'd never been close, and her fixation on him was setting off alarm bells in my mind.

"Damn it, Kat. You couldn't make this easy for once, could you?" Mari reached into the pocket of her bloodied lab coat and pulled out a black sphere about the size of a baseball. "I can't go back there without him, and I really didn't want to have to resort to this, but I swear I don't have a choice." She lobbed the black orb up to me, saying, "Catch!"

I reacted instinctively, reaching out to catch the thing with my right hand even as my mind screamed, *NO!* Because the orb was made of *anti-At*.

"No . . ." I gaped down at my hand, paralyzed by mind-numbing horror. Any second now, the *anti-At* would start soaking into my skin with a sickening tingling sensation.

Fuck. I'd gone and done it again. I just killed myself with my own stupidity and caught the damn orb of death. And thanks to me, Nik was nowhere in sight. This time, death—unmaking—would stick. And the damage to the timeline would be astronomical, because I'd been involved, however accidental or unwilling, in a lot of important, world-forming shit. If I disappeared from existence, everything I'd done since the day I was born would be undone.

"Where's Nik?" Mari asked, on her feet now, fists on her hips and stare intense. "Call him. He'll drop whatever he's doing and come running to save you."

"What?" I stared at the black orb, horrified and disgusted with myself, then gaped at Mari. "Why, Mars?" I looked at her, eyes stinging. "*Why?*" We hadn't been close in years, but we'd been inseparable once. She was like a sister to me. I'd *trusted* her.

"Please, Kat." She wrung her hands. "Call Nik. He'll fix this."

I blinked away tears, the chaos that had clouded my mind finally clearing enough that coherency returned, at least a little. "You need him." I cleared my throat, eyes narrowing. "That's what this has all been about. Your questions about me and him and the Senate . . . you telling me—*us*—to come check out this shipment . . ." I shook my head slowly. "God, I really am an idiot."

"Your words . . ."

I glanced down at my hand. Why wasn't it tingling? Last

time, when her *anti-At* blade had been buried deep in my side, I'd felt the particles working through me like tiny, soul-consuming insects. But this time, I felt nothing but the slightly warm surface of the orb against my shimmering skin.

My eyes widened as I registered what I was seeing. The ancient goddess tattoo in my skin—she'd extended one of her wings, the iridescent feathers extending onto my palm, an unbroken barrier of *At* between myself and the *anti-At* orb. She was protecting me.

I looked at Mari, my lips curving into a grin. A low, deep laugh spilled forth. "Would you look at that . . ."

Mari stared at my hand, disbelief written all over her face.

"Not today, bitch," I hissed, then chucked the orb into the water. It was relatively harmless out there, and I hoped the Puget Sound's current would carry it away to unknown depths where, in all likelihood, it would never have the chance to unmake anyone's soul again.

A slow, wicked smile spread across Mari's face. She looked better now, like she'd healed some—or maybe she just hadn't been that injured to begin with. Dom was still unconscious . . . still badly wounded. I frowned. He should've been regenerating. He should look better, too. But he didn't.

"Do you have any idea what you just—"

"Oh, shut up already," I spat, cutting Mari off as I drew my sword. Mercy sang out, a clear, pristine sound as her solidified *At* blade slid free of its steel sheath. It glimmered, almost glowing in the faint moonlight. I jumped down from the container, rolling on my landing and immediately settling into a defensive crouch a dozen feet from Mari. I didn't know why she'd betrayed me, but I knew how she would pay.

Mari stood with her feet shoulder width apart, twin black daggers as long as her forearms gripped in either hand. They appeared out of nowhere. "I don't want to fight you, Kat."

"Then don't," I said, lunging at her.

She raised her daggers, crossing them to block my sword. Her shorter blades met mine in a shower of glittering sparks of every conceivable color. The only thing as strong as *At* was *anti-At*. Our blades were evenly matched, even if *we* weren't. I'd always been the better fighter.

"I said I didn't *want* to fight you," Mari said through gritted teeth. "Not that I won't."

14

I was beating her. With every strike and parry, Mari weakened, and I drew closer to landing a lethal blow. She had to have known that if it came down to the two of us fighting, this was how it would end. So why set up some elaborate trap—and a shoddy one, at that—just to get to Nik? What did she need from him?

I blocked both of Mari's blades with my sword, twisting my own blade so hers tangled. She cried out, dropping one. I kicked her in the abdomen, launching her back a solid six feet. She skidded on her ass and dropped her other dagger, freeing up both hands to catch herself.

I stalked toward her, stopping just beyond her feet. I wasn't dumb enough to stand over her—not when she could materialize a new *anti-At* weapon in the blink of an eye. "Tell me why you're doing this," I said, staring down at her, sword at the ready should she try to lash out. "Why are you helping *them*? Did you really get caught, or was that all a lie, too?" For all I knew, she was the one responsible for Dom's current condition.

Mari laughed bitterly but said nothing.

"Tell me!"

"I bet you can't guess what's in that little sphere."

"I don't give two shits what's in the—"

"Dom's *ba*." She brought her hand up to her mouth, gasping dramatically. "But—oh, no! You threw it into the Sound! Now how will he ever be whole again?" She blinked, eyes wide and innocent. Mocking. "He won't be able to regenerate without it, that's for sure. And with his injuries . . ."

I shot the quickest glance at the open shipping container, suddenly more terrified for Dom's life than I'd ever been before.

Not quick enough. Mari struck, knocking my sword to the side and stabbing something into my belly.

I looked down, shocked to see her hand around the glistening black handle of a brand-new *anti-At* dagger, plunged to the hilt into my abdomen. It hurt like a bitch, stealing my breath even as the pain made me gasp. But even worse than the pain was the tingling. I could feel the miniscule *anti-At* particles separating from the blade and soaking into me, binding with my *ba*—my soul. I could feel myself being *unmade*.

"I'm sorry, Kat," Mari said, face twisted and eyes pleading. She seemed absolutely genuine, all mocking nonchalance from a moment earlier gone. Had it been an act? Or was *this* the act? "I didn't want this, I swear, but you didn't give me a choice. Call Nik and tell him to come here. He can save you." Gingerly, she pulled the dagger free and tossed it away, then eased me down to the ground with an arm around my waist.

Why? Why was getting Nik to come here so important to her that she'd risk changing the world as we knew it by unmaking me? The possible reasons were too slippery, and I could focus only on one thing. Nik. I needed him. He could save me.

I sucked in a shuttering breath. "I—I don't have—" I squeezed my eyes shut and clenched my jaw to fend off the pain. "—his number."

Mari knelt on the ground beside me. "Well, where is he?

You said he reached out to you—I know he wouldn't just let you run off on your own."

Lying on my back, right hand covering my stab wound, I stared at her. Now that the end was in sight, I was just glad that I wasn't alone. Her presence was oddly comforting, even though she was responsible for my impending death. "W— what makes you say th—that?"

"Because he knows you too well. You're rash, especially when your heart's actually in the fight." She shook her head, her eyes filled with sadness. "You let your emotions get in the way. You always have." She squeezed my shoulder. "Where do you think he is? I'll track him down. We can still save you."

Tears welled in my eyes. I tried to blame the pain, but they'd only started after I'd heard the genuine concern in Mari's voice . . . seen it in her shadowed jade eyes. "You're th—the one who d—did this." I inhaled shakily. "Why do you c— care?"

"Because I love you, idiot." She combed matted hair out of her face with dirty fingers. "God, you're such a moron sometimes."

I stared at her, wide-eyed and dumbstruck. And dying. Worse. Being unmade.

"Where's Nik, Kat? Please, you must have some idea."

I narrowed my eyes, not trusting that this wasn't all another act. "How do I know y—you'll come back?" I tried to shift my body into a more comfortable position, but it only served to sharpen the twisting pain in my gut. "You know I'll c—come after you."

She shrugged. "I'll chance it. But what I can't risk is letting you get unmade. You've played too big of a part in shaping our world into what it is today. Who knows what it would've become without you?"

I coughed a laugh. "One w—way to find out . . ."

"That's not going to happen." Mari loomed over me. "Where is he?"

I stared into her green eyes for long seconds, weighing my options. There weren't many. "The troll," I finally said. I wasn't positive, but it was my best guess. "In Fremont." I switched hands, my right so coated in blood it wasn't doing any good anymore. "He's probably there." *With Garth* . . . The thought felt important, but my sluggish, blood-deprived brain couldn't figure out why. "If not—maybe my apartment."

"Alright, it's a start." She stood and started jogging away. "Don't go anywhere," she called over her shoulder, a cell phone already at her ear. "I *will* come back for you." I never even had a chance to find out why all of this was happening.

Mari was out of sight by the time I realized my palm was burning even worse than before. The searing pain became so intense it muted the stab wound to a dull ache. I pulled my hand away from the wound and held it over my face. The tattoo of the Eye of Horus had changed; it still shimmered with that otherworldly iridescence of *At*, but now shining onyx streaks spread throughout the symbol like veins in marble.

"What the hell?"

And then it hit me—the tingling caused by the poisonous *anti-At* had stopped. It was gone.

The obsidian streaks in the tattoo had to be the *anti-At*, pulled from me, body and soul, by the Eye of Horus. I stared in awe at the thing that had just saved my life. That had just saved my whole damn existence. Protection amulet indeed.

The burning in my palm subsided and the streaks settled, the *anti-At* particles bound to the *At* in the ink, and I was left lying there with an ordinary stab wound. It was the kind of injury I could easily heal from. The kind I could deal with later.

There were more urgent matters to attend to.

Gingerly, I pushed myself up to a sitting position and un-zipped my left jacket pocket. I fished out my phone with fingers slimy with blood and dialed 9-1-1.

The phone rang twice before an emergency dispatcher picked up. "Nine-one-one, what's your emergency?"

"I need an ambulance." I clutched my side, gritting my teeth. "My friend—"

"State your name, please."

"My friend's dying," I snapped. "He needs help, *now!*"

"Where are you, ma'am?"

"Harbor Island—Terminal 18. There's a man in a shipping container—slot A-27. It's the second container up, so they'll need a ladder." I brushed my hair back from my face, cringing when strands pulled from sticking in the drying blood on my hand. "Just hurry, please!"

"Alright, ma'am, we're on our way. I need you to stay with your friend until—"

I hung up the phone and shoved it back into my pocket. Gritting my teeth, I pulled my legs in and, ever so carefully, stood. I lifted my sword, hilt-first, with the toe of my boot, then bent down part of the way to pick it up. I strained against the pain to sheath it over my shoulder and hobbled to the edge of the shore of the artificial island to search the smooth, black and silver surface of the water for the *anti-At* orb.

It took me nearly ten minutes to find it, and by the time I spotted Dom's *ba* bobbing along on the water's surface, I could hear the approaching sirens. I dove into the water and swam to the orb, my heavy boots becoming leaden in the water and doing their damnedest to drag me down. I grabbed it with my left hand, trusting the Eye of Horus would protect me again, and crawl-stroked to the dock on the opposite side of the waterway, muscles fatigued, lungs straining, and side burning with pain. Staying afloat became so difficult that for a minute there, I doubted I would make it.

It took an insane amount of effort, but I managed to pull myself up onto the dock behind a massive container ship. I flopped onto my back, giving myself a chance to catch my breath before the police and paramedics arrived. I needed to be gone before they had a chance to spot me and drag me in for questioning. There was somewhere else I needed to be. I had to find a way to get to Nik before Mari found him. I had no idea why she was so desperate to get her hands on him, but if it had anything to do with Ouroboros and whatever they were up to, it couldn't be anything good.

Garth's at the troll, too. Again, I had the nagging sense that *that* piece of information was important, but I couldn't quite put my thumb on the reason why.

I stared up at the stars, realization a bright burst in my mind, and I suddenly understood. I may not have had Nik's number, but I had Garth's. Or, at least, I had a way to contact Garth. I'd just used it.

I fumbled with my left pocket, pulling out my phone once more. It was dead, killed by the dip in the water.

"Oh, for fuck's sake," I grumbled, sitting up. The searing pain in my side was lessening—probably not because it was already healing, but because my brain was normalizing the sensation. I was getting used to it. Worked for me.

I climbed to my feet using one of the ship's thick dock lines, took a deep breath, and stumble-jogged back to the Ducati. It was the fastest I could go.

15

The nearest pay phone I could find was four blocks east in the Industrial District outside of a twenty-four-hour convenience store. The clerk working the graveyard shift watched me through the front windows. I guess a drowned-rat motorcycle chick dripping blood on the pavement is quite the sight to see. I turned my back to him as I dialed 9-1-1.

Three rings this time before the dispatcher picked up. "9-1-1, what's your emergency?" I was fairly certain it was the same woman I'd spoken to earlier.

I cleared my throat and made an effort to deepen my voice. "I have reason to believe one of your officers is in trouble. I need you to connect me to—"

"What is your name?"

"You've got to be fucking kidding me." I leaned my forehead against the inside of the phone's metal privacy alcove. "Officer Garth Smith is in trouble, and I need to talk to him *right now.*"

"Officer Smith has already called for backup. What is your name and how did you know he would be in trouble?"

"He already called for backup?" I went cold all over. Had Mari called in some Ouroboros goons to help her capture Nik? Would they hurt Garth? Would they go so far as to kill him? "Then it's too late," I said numbly, and hung up.

I stood there for a moment, feeling slightly nauseated, then took a deep breath and fished my sodden wallet out of my jacket's interior pocket before going into the 7-Eleven. Standing there being worried and afraid and feeling sorry for myself wouldn't help anyone. I headed straight for the refrigerated case of energy drinks in the back of the store, pulled two oversized cans out, and brought them up to the checkout counter. "No change," I said, dropping a soggy five on the counter before walking out through the door.

If there was one thing I'd learned during my years as one of the Senate's assassins, it's that carrying cash is one of the best ways to keep a low profile. I always have some on me. And since many of my current clients paid in cash, I almost never had to go to the bank.

I chugged the first can of sugar and caffeine in thirty seconds flat. I tossed it into the garbage can by the door, then cracked open the second and downed it in five big gulps. They should sustain me for at least an hour, even with the untended stab wound. When I crashed, I would land hard, but this bought me some time.

I hopped back onto my bike and kicked the engine on, zooming away from the convenience store. I made it to Fremont in barely ten minutes—record time—only slowing once I was within two blocks of the troll. I couldn't hear any sirens, but I could see the emergency vehicle's lights flashing off trees and the sides of houses up ahead.

I rode around a corner and pulled the Ducati up onto the sidewalk, killing the engine and backing it into the driveway of a dumpy-looking house with an overgrown yard. I left the bike tucked between a broken-down pickup raised up on cinder blocks and a rusted boat trailer and snuck out to the sidewalk, sticking to the shadows by the bushes and trees.

I had a good vantage point from behind the trunk of a

massive pine about halfway up the block. I could see the five police cruisers pulled up haphazardly around the underpass the Fremont Troll called home. An ambulance was just being loaded with a gurney, and if my eyes were right—and they almost always were—Garth was the injured guy strapped in, face covered by an oxygen mask. My heart sank.

I didn't know why Mari'd attacked him, but I was just relieved she hadn't killed him outright. But don't get me wrong, the relief didn't come close to surpassing the fury burning through my veins. Garth was innocent in all this, and he was, in a sense, my friend. Or the closest thing I had to a friend right now. He didn't deserve this. I'd pay Mari back for what she'd done to him.

I scanned the rest of the people milling around, looking for Nik's lanky silhouette. But all I saw were cops and paramedics and about a dozen lookie-loos. More civilians were trickling in from around the neighborhood. I searched the streets and yards around the underpass but saw no retreating figure. Which meant Mari must've found Nik. But had she taken him by force, or had he gone willingly once he'd heard I was in danger? Or was Nik injured, too?

My anger spiked. Hands in fists, I closed my eyes and took several long, deep breaths. Mari had said I had a tendency to act rashly and let my emotions take over. She viewed that as a weakness; I never had. She was about to bear the brunt of that rashness firsthand.

Hearing a person walk up the sidewalk just a few yards away, I opened my eyes and slunk deeper into the shadows. I couldn't stay here.

I supposed I knew where Mari and Nik would be headed— back to Harbor Island to "save" me—and I played with the idea of following them back there. But there were bound to be police crawling all over the place by now, thanks to my 9-1-1 call. Mari wouldn't risk it, and she would assume I'd ducked out as soon as the cops arrived.

Head hanging and hands in my coat pockets, I headed back to my bike. There was no real reason for me to track Nik and Mari down right away. She needed Nik for something—not that I knew what—and I figured he was safe enough for now. Besides, they'd be too preoccupied searching for me to get started on whatever plans she had for him. Dom was the one most urgently in need of help.

Back on the motorcycle, I pulled out of the little hideaway and wound around the block until I was merging onto Aurora Avenue to head back downtown to Harborview Medical Center. It was the city's most renowned trauma hospital, and there was no doubt in my mind that the paramedics would've taken Dom there.

By the time I turned off the bike in the hospital's parking garage, the glowing green digits on my little dashboard clock said it was just after ten at night. I parked the bike near the skybridge and hopped off. I shed my visible weapons, stashing them in a nearby garbage can that was nearly empty—under the bag, of course—and followed the signs to the skybridge. Visiting hours must've ended a while ago, because the garage was nearly empty.

I stopped in the third-floor bathroom near the elevators to clean up. My clothes were still soaked through, the *anti-At* orb containing Dom's *ba* bulging in my left coat pocket, and my hair was a tangled mess. Whatever scrapes or bruises I'd acquired during the fight were all but healed by now, though the wound in my abdomen still throbbed in time with my pulse and seeped blood with every intake of breath.

I folded up a wad of paper towels and pressed them against

the wound, wrapping my belt around my torso to hold the bundle in place. At least Mari'd had the decency to stab me below the hem of my tank top, leaving my shirt intact.

I zipped up my leather coat and stared at my reflection in the mirror. There was nothing I could do about the wet clothes, or about the eau de harbor water wafting off me, a delightful scent that would only get better. "Well, I think this is as good as it's going to get," I told my reflection. The girl in the mirror was a sorry copy of me, and I stuck my tongue out at her.

It was easy enough to find the emergency room—they're always on the ground floor, at least in every hospital I've ever been to. Convincing the intake nurse to share any information with me about Dom was more on the difficult side.

"Listen . . ." I let the sorrow and fear and dread I'd been feeling since first finding out about Dom's disappearance well up in the form of tears. My chin trembled, and when I spoke again, the quaver in my voice wasn't on purpose. "He's my brother. I just want to be here for him when he wakes up." I wiped a tear from my cheek with my knuckle. "*If* he wakes up . . ."

Finally—*finally*—the nurse took pity on me. Her entire demeanor softened and a warm, motherly glow shone in her eyes. "Alright, hon." She turned in her chair and stood, coming around the partition. "He's in surgery right now, but you can go back to the family waiting area." She held out an arm toward a doorway leading to a bustling emergency room filled with bay after curtained bay of patients in various stages of checking in and being treated.

She guided me through that chaotic room to another area beyond, where chairs, large potted plants, and an enormous fish tank had been arranged to delineate a "waiting area" within a larger open space at the convergence of several hallways. There were magazines on little end tables and arranged in a wooden display stand and not much else.

"There are vending machines around that corner, there," the nurse said, pointing across the open space. "And I'm not sure how long he'll be in surgery, but the cafeteria opens again at six in the morning."

"Is there a phone? I need to call my family," I said, voice catching. God, Heru was going to be pissed when he found out about all of this, specifically that I'd gotten involved in Nejeret matters without talking to him first. And Lex—she was, quite possibly, even closer with Dom than I was. She was going to kill me.

"Of course," the nurse said, pointing to a plant at one corner of the waiting area. "It's just on that table, there, hidden by the plant. You go ahead." She bustled away. "I'm going to check in with the doctors working on your brother . . . tell them he has family waiting so they know to update you if there's any news."

I nodded, feet dragging as I walked into the waiting area. The boost from the two energy drinks was depleting quickly, and I could feel the pull of regenerative sleep. It was tempting to give in—my wound would heal much faster then—but I'd be knocked out until my body determined it was recovered enough and ready for sustenance. I couldn't shake the feeling that if I gave in to the pull, something would happen to Dom, but if I could hold on to consciousness with my much lesser wound, then he could hold on to life.

I plopped down in the chair by the phone and picked up the receiver. It was one of the old corded phones with real buttons you could actually push. I dialed the only number I could think of that would get me to my family back on Bainbridge.

The line rang several times before anyone picked up. She probably wouldn't answer; it was an unrecognized number, after all, and it was late, especially for the mother of a three-year-old. I thought the call was going to go to voice mail, so I reached out my other hand to press the phone's hang-up mechanism.

"Hello?" Lex said after the fifth ring.

My voice stuck in my throat.

"Hello? Is anyone there?"

I licked my lips and swallowed roughly. "Lex?" My eyes stung, tears breaking free almost immediately. This was why I stayed away from the people I loved. This stupid, overwhelming vulnerability.

The line was quiet for a few seconds. "Kat? What's wrong?" Because for me to call her now, after nearly three years of radio silence, it had to be something bad.

Well, damn it, it was.

"You guys need to come to Harborview . . . Aset and Neffe need to come here." I cleared my throat, hoping Heru's twin sister and daughter, the two oldest, most skilled doctors I knew, would be able to do something for Dom even if the surgeons here couldn't. They had over ten thousand years of combined experience going for them, so the odds were in their favor. "It's Dom . . ."

Lex didn't respond for several more seconds, but I could hear her voice, muffled as though she'd pressed the phone to her shirt. And then she was back, clear as day. "We're on our way."

16

The hours passed in that waiting area in a blur, my mind trying its hardest to float away to the land of dreams while I did my damnedest to make sure that didn't happen. I guzzled far more vending machine coffee in a couple-hour period than was safe. Add to that the packaged cookies and little brownie bites I kept scarfing down, and I was feeling increasingly nauseated, my heart jackhammering against my sternum and my hands shaking even as my eyelids drooped.

Eventually, the call of regenerative sleep was too much for the battalion of sugar and caffeine or the discomfort of the belt pressing into my injury and pinching the skin of my waist. I passed out, curled up on the chair by the phone, and was, for some unknown period of time, dead to the world.

The scent of grease and fried potatoes filled my nose, luring me out of a dreamless sleep. I groaned, not understanding how I'd come to be lying down or why my belt wasn't pinching my skin.

"I knew that would work." The voice was feminine and more than a little smug. I recognized it immediately.

"Lex?" I cracked my eyelids open to see a pair of white fast-food bags with the familiar orange and blue Dick's Drive-In logo across the side, stuffed so full of glorious fast food that the paper bags were bulging. Lex's face was beside them, her head tilted to the side, her strange, crimson eyes mere inches from mine.

"Hey, Kit-Kat." Her lips curved into a hesitant smile. "How are you feeling?" She brushed a strand of hair from my eyes with gentle fingertips. She still treated me like her kid sister, even though I was technically about twenty years older than her due to a ridiculously complicated time travel situation. I didn't really mind, though. It was actually kind of nice that she remembered me the way I used to be.

I pushed myself up from the string of chairs I'd stretched out on while asleep, moving the warm bags of greasy burgers and fries to the seat next to me, and rubbed my eyes. "Better," I told her.

Peering down at myself, I pulled up my tank top a few inches to get a look at the stab wound. My belt was gone—coiled up on the floor nearby—and a neat gauze bandage had replaced the blood-crusted wad of paper towels.

"Aset cleaned you up when we first got here, while Neffe was in conferring with Dom's doctors," Lex explained. She moved the fast-food bags closer to me. "You should eat. You're too thin." It wasn't a judgment, just a statement of the aftereffects of Nejeret regeneration. My body had diverted all possible resources to healing me, including drawing from any stored energy, namely fat.

I huffed out a breath. "And here I was hoping to pick up a few years for a couple days . . . see what it's like to be a real-life grown-up." I dug into the first paper bag, pulling out a cheeseburger wrapped in foil paper and tearing it open, stomach rumbling. I was ravenous.

Lex laughed softly, but no hint of mirth touched her eyes. "I got you a strawberry milkshake, too," she said, her gaze flicking to the table with the phone, where two Dick's cups awaited me. "And a Cherry Coke."

I grabbed the latter, taking a deep pull from the straw. The sweet, fizzy liquid helped me get the burger down in three bites. I unwrapped a second as soon as the first was nothing but crumbs. "Thanks," I said around a mouthful.

She nodded and stood, not the least bit disturbed by my pig-out session. She knew my hunger as well as any Nejeret who'd been injured enough to go through regeneration cycles. She crossed the waiting area to sit in a chair beside her husband, Heru. I was studiously avoiding looking at him. I knew what I'd find if I did—that haughty, hawkish stare, his burnished gold eyes focused on me, and his expression a cold, emotionless mask. Painfully beautiful, just like his sister's and his nephew's faces, but giving nothing away.

"So, what happened?" It was Lex who asked first, despite Heru's eyes searing the question into my skin. "To Dom," she said. "And to you."

I could only stand to look at her for a few seconds. I didn't see blame in her garnet eyes, but that didn't stop me from feeling it. My gaze quickly diverted to the floor, seeking out the pale stains no amount of carpet cleaner could remove from the mutely patterned ivory and blue rug.

"Explain," Heru said, the one word an iron-clad command. It was the first time I'd heard his voice in years, but his faint, slightly Middle Eastern accent was exactly as I remembered it. As was the power he could wield with his voice alone.

He was a Senate member, elected by our people along with Aset and Lex. But he was more than that, too—the leader of my clan and the general to our people. He'd been the former for more than twenty years, since I swore an oath forsaking my clan of birth for his, and the latter for over four thousand years.

Power wafted off him in waves, and he had more charisma and charm than anyone I'd ever met, though he could turn it off like flipping a switch. I never understood how Lex could do it, *be* with him. But somehow she managed, and not as a doormat, but as his equal. His partner.

I locked eyes with Heru. It was a mistake, because once he had me, I couldn't look away. My hands stilled, a half-unwrapped cheeseburger sitting on my lap.

I considered lying to him about everything that had happened over the last few days. For all of two seconds. "Nik came to me," I confessed. "He told me Dom was missing and asked me to look into it because, you know . . ." Actually, I realized that maybe they *didn't* know; I'd been keeping my distance for so long. Which then made me wonder how Nik had known in the first place. I made a mental note to pry the truth out of him later before starting my explanation. "My *sheut*," I said, "the way it's developed—well, it makes it so the things I draw have power." I continued unwrapping the burger, hands shaking a little. How could they not be, when Heru was staring at me so . . . stare-y. "In some ways, it's like they're *alive*."

I took a bite of the burger, considering the quickest and easiest way to explain what I could do and how and why Nik thought I'd be able to find Dom and the other missing Nejerets when nobody else could. "There was this case about a year and a half ago—a missing sixteen-year-old girl. The cops weren't having any luck, and the older sister came into the shop, wanting to get the girl's name tattooed on her wrist." I took another bite, washing it down with a sip of Cherry Coke. "She got to talking, and one thing led to another, and my sketches of the girl's name started taking on a life of their own, changing and spelling out different things."

I set down the cup by the phone on the end table. "I called

in an anonymous tip as soon as the girl's sister left, and they found the girl later that day. She was a little worse for wear, but she was alive. Some sick fuck had abducted her and was 'training' her to be sold as a sex slave." I glanced down at the burger, momentarily too disgusted for even my ravenous post-regeneration hunger. "That's how my side business of finding people started."

"So, you're a PI?" Lex asked.

I shrugged, shaking my head. "I don't have a license or anything, and I don't advertise, but people still come to me. Word of mouth, I guess." I thought of Garth and the missing street kids. "Some of the cops have even heard about me now." I hoped Garth was all right, but my fear for Dom's life far surpassed my concern for Garth. Even so, I thought I might get up and wander the hospital in search of him in a bit. It would be nice to stretch my legs, and seeing that he was really all right—*if* he was all right—would set at least part of my mind at ease.

Heru exchanged a quick glance with Lex. "And Nik knew about this?" he asked. *How?* was unspoken, but implied.

I swallowed and nodded, just as in the dark about the *how* of that reality as he was. "He came to me a few nights ago," I said. "Told me about Dom and the others. I did some readings and sketches, and I have this wall—" I waved a hand to the side dismissively. "It doesn't matter." After a deep inhale, I continued, "I kept seeing the same symbol over and over. And then this cop got involved, and I realized the missing Nejerets are linked to a bunch of street kids who've gone missing over the past couple months."

"A cop?" Lex asked, at the same time as Heru said, "What symbol?"

I couldn't ignore Heru's question. He was a man whose

passive greatness was so stifling that if you told some random human that he was a god, nine times out of ten they'd shrug and nod, admitting it was a possibility. "A snake eating its own tail," I told him. "It helped me link the disappearances to the Ouroboros Corporation."

Heru's golden tiger eyes narrowed.

"Mari's working with them," I said. "Did you know that?"

Lex's mouth fell open, and Heru shook his head ever so faintly.

"So, yeah . . . she's not 'missing.'" I gripped the side of my abdomen, still aching dully from the stab wound. "She's the one who did this. I'm pretty sure she has Nik . . . and she managed to get me with an *anti-At* dagger."

"*What?*" Lex was standing before the word was out of her mouth.

"I'm fine," I said, holding out my left hand, emblazoned with the black-veined Eye of Horus. "Turns out my sheut's good for more than just drawing pictures, reading fortunes, and finding people . . ."

Lex moved closer, crouching and eyes squinting as she studied my palm. "What *is* that?"

"*At* ink," I told her. "Nik made it." I shrugged out of my jacket and set it on the chair beside me. "It's what these are, too. The only permanent ink there is for a Nejeret."

"And it protected you?" Lex asked, looking from my hand to my face and back.

I nodded vehemently. "And that's not all it did." I remembered the way it had itched, then burned, when Mari had first emerged from the container. "I think it tried to warn me that I was in danger—I just didn't know it." I stared hard at Lex. "You guys should seriously consider letting me ink you with one of these bad boys. Could save your life . . ."

"I'll think about it," she said with a frown.

I looked at Heru. God or not, it was my turn to spear him with a hard stare. "How'd this all happen? How did you *let* it? And how the hell did the Senate *not* know what Ouroboros was up to?" Not that I really had any clue what exactly they were up to, just that it involved abducting Nejerets and human kids and apparently tearing the *bas* out of their Nejeret captives. "Even Nik's been paying attention to them. He said their 'life extension' products seemed fishy."

"For some time," Heru said, "it has been my belief that there is corruption within the Senate." Irritation tensed his exotic features. It was the most emotion I'd seen in him in years. Then again, this was the first time I'd seen him in years.

I scoffed. "You think?" I'd sensed that vein of corruption the day they tasked me, a nineteen-year-old freshly manifested Nejeret who just happened to be invisible in the echoes thanks to the *first* time Mari stabbed me with an *anti-At* dagger, with hunting down and eliminating their enemies.

Heru's responding stare put mine to shame. "All of this stays between us."

"I literally talk to *no one*." At least, no one who mattered to them. "Who do you think I'll tell? My receptionist?"

The corner of Heru's mouth twitched like he was holding in his amusement, but Lex frowned.

At the sound of footsteps coming from the hallway leading to Dom's operating room, all three of us swiveled our heads. Neffe approached, scrubs smudged with crimson bloodstains, dark hair held back by a blue cap tied behind her head, and a surgeon's mask pulled down below her chin to reveal her striking face.

Born during the most famous ancient Egyptian period, the New Kingdom's Eighteenth Dynasty, to Queen Hatshepsut and the great god Heru—the very same Heru sitting in the waiting area with me—Neffe was a stunning vision of a woman. And her brain was even better; her intellect and skill as a healer was nearly unmatched. Though her personality left something to be desired.

"How is he?" Lex asked, taking a step toward Neffe, hands wringing. Lex, Dom, and I shared a father, and she and Dom had always had a special bond.

Neffe took hold of Lex's hands, showing more compassion than I'd have thought her capable of. "It is not good, I'm afraid. Aset is still in there, leading the team, but . . ." She shook her head, her honey eyes filled with sorrow. She and Dom had been a part of each other's lives for centuries, so I don't know why it surprised me so much that she actually gave a shit about him. But it did. "He's not healing. No matter what we do, it's like working on a patient with a severe autoimmune disease—the exact opposite of what should be happening."

I opened my mouth, then snapped it shut again. Surely I hadn't skipped over the part about Dom's *ba* having been torn out of his body, had I? I quickly reviewed our conversation so far in my mind, and much to my shame, I had. "It's his *ba*," I said, standing and retrieving the *anti-At* orb out of my left pocket, then holding it out for the others to see. Neffe reached for the shimmering black orb, and I quickly drew it back to me. "Don't touch it!"

Neffe pulled her hand back. "Is that—"

"*Anti-At?*" I said. "Yes."

Her eyes rounded. "But how are you—"

"It's a long story," I said with a huff. "The point is, Dom's *ba* is in here, courtesy of Mari. Is there any way you can get it out of here and back into him?"

"Short of a needle made of *anti-At* . . ." Neffe shook her

head. "No, I don't believe so. Not even Nik would be able to break through it." She turned and started back toward the hallway. "This changes things. I'll return shortly with a new assessment of the situation."

I went to stuff the orb back into my pocket, but Lex grabbed my wrist. "Is that really him in there?" she asked, bringing her face close to its poisonous surface.

I pulled free from her gentle hold. "So Mari claims . . ."

"Can he hear us?" Lex asked, straightening as her eyes moved from the orb to my face and back.

I lifted one shoulder and shook my head. "I honestly don't know."

"Mari did this?" From the hard glint in Lex's eyes, I wagered that Mari—whatever reasoning she'd had behind splintering Dom's body and soul—was about to get far more than she'd bargained for. Heru was shit-scary when he wanted to be. But if there was one person I didn't ever want to piss off, it was Lex. She'd been through hell traveling through time across millennia to get back to us, and she knew what it meant to lose everything. I mean, come on—the woman birthed the two new, true gods of our universe.

And she loved Dom as much as anyone. Maybe more. If there was anyone I pitied right now, it was Mari. She was in for a universe of hurt.

17

I'm not used to sitting still without having something to do. I've always got a pen in hand, a tattoo machine, or my tarot cards. I had none of those things in the hospital waiting area, and once the food was gone, it was painfully dull, which only increased my anxiety about Dom. If only I had my cards . . . but then they'd have taken a dip with me in the waterway, and I doubted even their magic ink would've survived that.

The minutes felt like hours, the hours like days. Not that I'd made it even a half hour sitting down there, doing nothing, but still . . .

I pushed up out of my chair maybe an hour after I woke to the scent of cheap burgers and fries. "I need to move," I said, reaching my hands over my head and arching my back in a stretch. Now was as good of a time as any to search for Garth. "I'm gonna walk around." I picked up my leather jacket off the chair. It wasn't cold in the hospital, but it wasn't toasty, either.

Lex's eyes moved to the jacket in my hands, then back to my face. "Oh, um, alright." Did she think I was ducking out? Not that I could blame her if she did. My track record was less than stellar in the slinking-away department.

I set the coat down, hoping doing so would do enough to reassure her that I really would come back. I did pull the *anti-At* orb from the pocket, though; I wasn't willing to leave that

behind with a bunch of Nejerets. To a human, it would be relatively safe—erasing them from the echoes, but nothing more,
since no *ba* connected them to that higher plane. But to a
Nejeret with a *ba*, it would unmake them, body and soul. Only
I had immunity, thanks to the Eye of Horus inked in *At* on my
hand.

Once the orb was out in the open again, Heru's eyes locked
onto it.

"I'll be back in a bit." I checked the clock on the wall. It
was nearly five in the morning. "The cafeteria opens soon.
Maybe we can grab breakfast when I get back?"

Lex nodded. "That sounds good."

I found the stairs and headed up a floor, wandering its hallways and corridors while I tossed and caught the orb, over and
over. I passed someone in scrubs every now and again, but
there weren't too many people around. Certainly not many visitors at this hour of the morning, and none of them cops,
which I figured would be the first sign that my hunt for Garth
was bearing fruit. Nobody seemed concerned about my presence, at least not once they caught sight of the bandage on my
abdomen. I supposed they thought I was a patient, even if I
wasn't wearing a hospital gown.

Harborview Medical Center is an enormous facility made
up of at least a dozen buildings, some connected, others standing on their own small block. I mostly just stuck to the main
cluster of five interconnected buildings. After I'd done a full
circuit of the second floor, I moved up to the third using the
same stairwell as before.

It spat me out into a waiting room filled with cops. I froze
in the doorway, heavy fire door propped open against my
shoulder. All eyes were on me.

Their scrutiny was so intense that I started to ease back

into the stairwell, but when my brain finally put two and two together and I realized this must be where Garth was being treated, I changed my trajectory. Slowly, I pushed through the door and into the waiting room. I spotted walrusy Officer Henderson sitting in the corner in jeans and a wrinkled blue polo. He was easy to recognize, even out of his uniform.

Henderson stood and I planted my feet, head held high, bolstering myself for the inevitable ejection from this apparently cop-only shindig. "I suppose you're looking for Garth?" he said as he drew near.

I nodded, my gaze flicking to the side at a whispered "Ink Witch." I ground my teeth together.

"Come on." Henderson waved me onward. "He's been asking for you."

My eyes widened, stinging as shame welled within me. It had taken me hours to come looking for Garth, I'd been so focused on Dom. Sure, I'd been passed out most of that time, but I certainly hadn't come as soon as I could've.

Henderson led me through the wide entrance into the intensive care unit. Lead settled in my stomach. It was my fault that Garth was here. The space was bustling with activity, and the incessant cacophony of arrhythmic beeping was enough to drive a Nejeret nuts.

We made a right, then a left, and Henderson stopped at the third doorway on the right. He reached into the room and knocked on the open door. "You decent, kid?"

"Why?" Garth said. "You looking for a show?"

My lips curved into a small smile at hearing his voice. He was alright.

Henderson laughed, a low, rough sound that came from his belly. "You've got a lady visitor."

"I said no strippers!"

Henderson gave me a questioning look.

I crossed my arms and raised one eyebrow. "I'm not a stripper."

"Kat?" Garth asked from within the room. "Is that you?"

After a deep breath—and another—I walked into the hospital room. Garth was propped up to a reclined sitting position, an entourage of beeping machines and IV bags on racks surrounding the upper half of his bed. His distinctive, noble features were mottled with bruises and cuts, and his hospital gown looked flimsy on his large frame.

"Hey," I said, forcing a lame smile.

He scanned me. "You look like crap."

I laughed. It only sounded slightly nervous. "Right back at you," I said with a halfhearted wink. I sat in the chair some visitor before me had left at his bedside.

"What happened?" he asked, his eyes searching my face. "When you didn't show up, I thought you'd pulled a fast one on me, but then your friend was there, and then we were jumped by that guy from—" He cleared his throat, then succumbed to a pretty painful-looking coughing fit.

I reached for the plastic cup and pitcher on his wheely tray and poured him a glass of water.

"Thanks," he said when he'd regained his voice. "I was afraid . . . I thought he must've gotten to you first."

I narrowed my eyes. "*He* who?" Maybe someone else who worked with Mari?

"The guy from the bar—you remember him, don't you? The bartender . . . ?"

The blood drained from my face, and I went cold all over. That fucking shitstain—I still didn't know his name—must've overheard Garth say "Nejeret" in the bar. I pressed my lips together and focused on breathing through the sudden spike of adrenaline. I would kill that fucker. It would be the first time I'd killed someone I'd had any kind of sexual involvement with, but that wouldn't stop me. My gaze strayed from Garth's as memories from that stairwell flashed through my mind, and silence stretched between us.

"Kat?"

I refocused on Garth. "How do you know what I am?" I asked, shooting a quick glance at the door. I had to know just how much he knew, just how dangerous he was—to my people, and to himself.

He was quiet for a moment, then cleared his throat. "Do you know anything of my people's history?" he said, so softly that I wouldn't have been able to hear him if I'd been human. His gaze met mine like he was waiting for an answer. Like he knew I'd heard him.

My eyes narrowed, just a little. "The Squamish? Some . . ." I knew what most kids who grow up in Seattle know: that the Squamish had been moved onto a reservation in the mid-1800s, and that their chief had been the famous Chief Sealth that Seattle was named for. I also knew a smidgen more—over a century ago, the Squamish helped a Nejeret who was lost in time: my half-sister, Lex.

"I changed my last name to Smith when I was in middle school," Garth said. "Kids can be cruel, and they thought I was trying to claim that I was the prince of Seattle because of my last name."

"Which is . . . ?"

"Seattle."

My eyebrows rose, and I leaned forward, resting my elbows on my knees. "So Chief Sealth was your—"

"Great-great-great-great-great-grandfather, yes," Garth said with a nod. He stared past me at the broad window. "And my family has passed down a certain secret history, one that belongs only to us." He sipped his water. "My people believe that everything has a spirit—the eagles and crows, the trees, the Puget Sound . . . even the land itself. One day, two centuries ago, the spirit of a doe took human form and tasked Sealth's grandfather with a sacred duty. He was to teach his children of this duty so they might be prepared when the day came."

I licked my lips, already guessing where this was going. "What was the duty?"

"A woman would arrive one day, another spirit, and she would need my family's help." He looked at me, *saw* me, and ever so quietly whispered, "Her name was Alexandra, and she was a Nejeret."

I stared at him, stunned into silence. He was so much more entangled in our history than I'd feared, and I was suddenly terrified that our burgeoning friendship would be the thing that brought the rage of the Senate crashing down on him and his family. I had to put some emotional distance between us, and I had to do it now.

"I did," I blurted, eyes locked with his. "Pull a fast one on you." I glanced down at my hands, fingers knotted together. "But I swear it was only to keep you *out* of danger, not to put you in it, and I'm *so* sorry."

"Oh." He sounded hurt. Good. Now I just had to make him see. Make him understand.

I forced myself to look at him. "I mean it, Garth. This thing that I'm investigating—it's bad. It's so much worse than anything you could've imagined, and I didn't want you to get drawn in any deeper. My world's not safe for people like—"

"Just stop," he said. Now it was his turn to purposely not look at me. "You should probably go."

"Garth—" Maybe I'd hurt him too much. If he wasn't willing to listen to me, he might be more of a danger to himself than he was before.

He turned his face further away from me. He wouldn't listen to me. Not right now. I'd have to find another way to make him listen. To make him understand just how important his silence was.

I nodded and stood, swallowing roughly. "Do you know what happened to Nik?" I asked.

Garth shook his head. "He was there when I blacked out, gone when I came to."

My nostrils flared. This was on me; I accepted that. But it was also on that damned bartender. And he would answer for it—just as soon as I'd dealt with Mari.

18

After leaving Garth's room, I headed back down to the waiting area. The moment I saw Lex, sitting there, looking generally miserable, I realized there was maybe one way I could get Garth to listen to me *and* lift my half-sister's spirits a bit.

"Hey, Lex," I said as I drew nearer. "There's something I want to show you."

She glanced at Heru, her hand settling on his knee. An unspoken conversation passed between them, and he nodded. She leaned in, kissing him on the cheek, then stood and smoothed down the front of her sweater and jeans.

"Come on," I said, leading her back the way I'd just come. "It's not far . . . just up a couple floors."

Lex looked over her shoulder, her lip pulled between her teeth and her brow furrowed.

"It won't take long," I promised. "Just trust me." I couldn't help the lilt of a question. I didn't know if she trusted me at all anymore. And if she did, I wasn't sure whether she should.

We emerged from the third floor stairwell into the waiting room packed full of police officers a couple minutes later. Lex looked around, eyebrows raised. I waved to Henderson, and he gave me a slight nod.

"Where are you taking me?" Lex asked, laughing nervously.

I grinned at her over my shoulder. "There's someone I want you to meet. Someone *you'll* want to meet."

We reached Garth's room, and I peeked around the door-frame. He was just as I'd left him, gaze focused on the window and the rain pouring down in sheets outside.

"Garth, there's—"

"I told you to—" His dismissal died out when he looked at me. Or rather, looked past me, no doubt at Lex. His focus returned to me, confusion lighting his brown eyes.

"Garth," I said, stepping into the room. I reached behind me, finding Lex's arm, and pulled her in after me. "This is my sister, Lex—Alexandra." It was the name his people had known her by when she'd passed through their land—and time—over a century and a half ago.

Garth's eyes bugged out.

I turned to Lex. "This is Officer Garth Smith, who changed his last name when he was in middle school . . . from *Seattle*. He's descended from Chief Sealth."

Lex's eyes narrowed, and a second later, her lips spread into a broad grin, her gaze sliding past me and landing on Garth. "You—" She moved further into the room to stand behind the chair at Garth's bedside. "How?" She looked from Garth to me and back.

"Chief Sealth's daughter, Kikisoblu, was my great-great-great-great-grandmother. I grew up hearing stories of you and your people, but I never really believed any of them until I met Kat." His eyes shifted to me. "I did some digging after our first meeting. I found your birth certificate." The corner of his mouth lifted, and he scanned me from head to toe, giving me an appreciative nod. "You look good for a thirty-eight-year-old."

Heat suffused my cheeks.

"I—" Lex shot me a questioning glance, and I nodded, letting her know that he knew exactly who she was—and *what* we were. "I knew Kikisoblu . . . not well, but she saved my life once when I was in a bit of a sticky situation. She was a remarkable woman. And Sealth . . ." She shook her head, laughing under her breath. "He was something else."

"This is unreal," Garth said.

"Truly incredible," Lex agreed. "Can I ask you—how many of your people know of us?"

"Just my family," Garth told her. "We've kept your secret, just as we promised all those years ago."

"Then you know how important it is that you continue to keep that secret a, well, *secret*," Lex said.

"Which means not telling every Nejeret you cross paths with that you know what they are," I added.

Alarm flashed across Lex's crimson eyes. "I can propose his name be added to the protected humans list, but there are no guarantees . . ."

Garth's expression turned quizzical.

"I'm pretty sure that's why you were attacked," I explained. "You know too much, and the wrong person found out. To the rest of the world, you have to pretend that we don't exist." I snorted out a breath. "It's probably best if you just forget about us."

"Kat!" Lex said, giving me a look of scandalized disbelief. She shook her head, her eyes narrowed, and laughed under her breath. When her attention shifted back to Garth, her features smoothed over. "I'd like to speak with you more, I really would," she said, "but I should get back downstairs. Our brother was the victim of a—well, he's in bad shape down in the ER. They're not sure if he'll . . ." Lex's voice seemed to catch in her throat. "We should get beck."

Garth looked at me, some measure of forgiveness in his gaze.

I risked the tiniest of apologetic smiles.

"You should go," he said. Though the words were the same ones he'd spoken earlier, they felt entirely different. "I'm not going anywhere for a while, so you know where to find me."

Lex started back across the room, but she stopped halfway and turned back to Garth. "Kat's right, though. This secret—what we are—it's dangerous . . ."

Garth's eyes shifted to Lex, then back to me. "So the Ink Witch keeps telling me."

I bristled. "You know, I really hate that name."

Garth chuckled. "I know."

Lex and I were halfway down the stairwell by the time she spoke again. "Ink Witch?"

I groaned. "It's a stupid nickname."

"Oh." She was quiet for a few seconds, but I could feel her sidelong stare on my face. "I think he likes you. But he's upset with you, too."

"He's in here because of me," I said. "Because of all this . . ." I shook my head as we started down the final flight of stairs. "I tried to keep him out of it, but it just made things worse." I considered telling her about the bartender, but I wanted to deal with him on my own, Senate agent or not. "I never should've visited him at the station. It would've have been best for him if he'd never met me at all."

Lex grabbed my wrist, pulling me to a halt halfway down the stairs. "Do you really think that?"

I eyed her. "It *would* have been best for him if he'd never met me. It's safer that way."

Lex shook her head, her brow furrowed. "You don't get to choose what's best for people, Kit-Kat. There's one person in this world that you're responsible for—*you*." She gave my wrist a tug, then let it go. "It's not your job—your *right*—to decide what's good or bad for other people." Her carmine eyes searched mine. "Don't you get that?"

I looked away, focusing on the wall.

"Like with your mom . . ." With those four words, it felt like she'd rammed me in the chest with a wrecking ball. "She made the choice that was best for her—trading her life for yours."

A tear leaked from the corner of my eye, and I jutted out my jaw to keep my chin from trembling. "If it weren't for me, she'd still be here."

"She chose your life over hers, Kat. *She* chose that, not you. You have to let her take ownership of that choice." Steel seeped into Lex's voice. "Stop making decisions for the people around you. We're all responsible for ourselves, for our choices. *We* love you, and you don't get to take that away just because it scares you. Because that love is *ours*, not yours."

I closed my eyes in a long blink, then looked at her. I had no words, just a shit-ton of long-dormant emotions all unfurling at once.

"Stop punishing yourself for your mom's choice. You've twisted it into something shameful in your head, but what she did was selfless; it was beautiful. Give her a little credit, for once in your life. Be proud that she was your mom . . . that you're *her* daughter. Be the legacy she deserves."

I looked up at the shiny, whitewashed cement ceiling. Tears streamed from the corners of my eyes.

"I'll give you a moment," Lex said, continuing down the stairs. "Come join us when you're ready."

"Yeah," I said, voice raspy. "Sure." I sunk down to sit on a stair and rested the side of my head against the metal railing.

"I'm sorry," I whispered. Because Lex was right. About

everything. I'd been an ass for the last two decades. Ever since my mom shoved me out of the way of the gun and took the bullet meant for me, I'd made it all about me—about my loss. But it wasn't. It was about her—her choice. Her sacrifice. Her gift.

As I sat in that stairwell, facing the things I'd been hiding from for all these years, it felt like the whole world shifted around me. Everything I'd believed was based on faulty logic. On a foundation of cardboard and Styrofoam. I'd been wrong—blind—and I was finally ready to accept it. I'd been in hiding from myself for twenty years, but not anymore. Never again.

19

When I emerged from the stairwell, Aset was standing near where Lex and Heru were sitting in the waiting area. As soon as I stepped onto the sitting area's rug, Aset stomped over to me, raised her hand, and slapped me. Hard.

I pressed my hand against my cheek and worked my jaw from side to side. While she might have been petite and pretty as all hell, Aset was ancient and had spent millennia training to be nearly as fierce and lethal as her twin brother. Who, at the moment, was watching from a chair, Lex's hand in his and the faintest smirk twisting his lips.

"I'm sorry about Nik," I said, assuming her anger was because her son seemed to be the latest Ouroboros victim. "I knew Mari wanted him for something, and I told her where he was to save my own life." And to keep this timeline from unraveling as the thread of my life disappeared, or so I'd thought at the time. I hadn't known there was another way.

"You're a foolish child," Aset said with a huff. Her rich, ancient accent was more pronounced than usual. "Nekure is more than capable of dealing with Mari."

My eyes narrowed. "Then why did you hit me?"

"Because I missed you." Her amber eyes shone. "For three years, you couldn't even be bothered to answer my calls, and you made it clear I was not welcome in your life. What was I to think? I had to resort to hiring a private investigator to check up on you."

My lips parted. "You did *what*?"

"Even Nekure checked in with me time and again, letting me know he was alive."

"Thanks for letting the rest of us know," Lex muttered under her breath.

I sniffed. So Aset hadn't shared her periodic phone calls with Nik with the rest of our unconventional family. Now who was the inconsiderate one? I opened my mouth to make that very point when the sound of footsteps came from the hallway leading to Dom's operating room.

Neffe appeared, crossing to the waiting area, shoulders slumped. "He went into cardiac arrest." She held up a hand to cut off our questions. "We managed to bring him back, and he's stable enough for the moment, but there's no way to predict how long that will last." She was quiet for a moment, her eyes locked with her father's. "I thought we could stabilize him, even without his *ba*, but . . ." She shook her head. "His organs are starting to shut down. There's nothing more we can do for him, and life support will keep him going for only so long. If we don't reunite him with his *ba* soon, he will die."

"Mari's the only one who can release his *ba* from that thing," Heru said, pointing to the inky black orb in my hand.

"But how can we find her, Father?" Neffe asked. "The Senate's been searching for Mari and the others for months . . ."

Heru's hawkish stare locked onto me. "She'll be looking for you if she truly believes you're infected with *anti-At*."

I nodded. "There's no way for her to know about this mark," I said, rolling the orb to my fingertips and flashing the black-streaked iridescent Eye of Horus on my palm. "So far as she knows, she *needs* to find me before this world changes into the wild unknown." I looked at Aset. "If Nik's with her, can't you just call him?"

She shook her head. "I tried that hours ago. His phone's either off or dead."

"If you made your whereabouts known to her," Heru said, "Mari would come to you."

I shook my head. "Not if she thinks you guys are around. She might prefer to preserve this timeline, but not at the expense of her own life." I frowned, considering another angle. "I think she's kind of a big shot at Ouroboros. If I walked in there alone, asked for her, and told them who I was, they'd be able to get the message to her."

"But that still doesn't get her *here*," Neffe said. "And there's no guarantee that she'll be willing to help." Neffe hesitated. "What about Mei? We could use her to coerce—"

"Out of the question," Aset said. Mei was Mari's adoptive mother. She was also Nik's only child—that I knew of—and Aset's only grandchild. She was technically dead, having been murdered during all the hoopla a couple decades ago, but being a time traveler—however grounded she currently was by the new gods' ban on time travel—she'd found a loophole to extend her life by jumping forward in time. Eventually, the day would come when she'd have to return and allow her own murder. But not yet.

"If I talk to Mari . . ." I licked my lips. She'd said she loved me; if that was true, she'd have to listen. "I don't know why she's doing all of this, but she's not a bad person. She'll help Dom. She'll make the right choice." I exchanged a look with Lex. Her red-rimmed eyes made her look a little shell-shocked. "I have to trust that she'll make the right choice."

Everyone looked at Heru, our people's general, an uncrowned king. Finally, he nodded solemnly. "If she chooses wrong—if she resists—I authorize you to use whatever force necessary to capture her and bring her here. This isn't how Dom ends. He's a warrior. He deserves better."

"I understand." I turned away from Heru and set the orb down on a chair, then picked up my leather jacket and put it on. I stuffed the orb back into my pocket and met Heru's fierce golden eyes. "This isn't how he ends," I agreed, meaning it with every fiber of my being.

This isn't how he ends.

20

I hurried back to the parking garage and found the trash can near my bike, where I'd stowed my weapons. The trash bag was still mostly empty, and it was easy enough to retrieve my things. Within minutes of reaching the garage, I was suited up once more and kicking my leg over the Ducati's high seat.

It was still early enough that the streets of downtown Seattle weren't crowded, only a single overnight road construction crew attempting to slow me down. Fourth Avenue was closed off, and instead of following the detour down to Third so I could swing back around on Fifth—damn one-way streets—I flipped a bitch and rode down Fifth going the wrong way. It was only a block and a half, and Dom's life was on the line.

A couple cars honked at me, and someone in a white BMW sedan rolled down their window to inform me none too politely that I was going the wrong way. I ignored them all and parked the bike on the sidewalk just a few feet from the Fifth Avenue entrance into the Columbia Center, not caring that the parking job was about as illegal as they get. I jumped off the bike, practically ripping my helmet off and dropping it on the cement, and ran to the door.

I entered the posh building on the second floor, all the mall shops still closed, doors shut and security gates pulled down. I could hear people down in the food court, though, early birds at the several cafes grabbing their morning coffee fixes.

A single woman was waiting at the elevator. I stopped a couple feet from her, crossed my arms over my chest, and met her eyes, forcing a half-assed smile. Her gaze slid to the sword strapped to my back, and her eyes rounded. She backed away slowly, then turned and jogged to the escalator. No doubt she was going in search of security or, even better, police. I sniffed and turned my back to the escalators. Some people are so jumpy.

Widening my stance, I rolled my head from side to side to crack my neck as I watched the digital counter over the elevator. *Eleven. Ten. Nine. Eight. Seven . . .*

The metallic clang of boots tromping up the escalator caught my attention, and I glanced over my shoulder. Two of Seattle's finest in their starched midnight-blue uniforms barreled up the moving stairway, one a chick, the other a dude.

I peered up at the counter. *Three. Two . . .*

Ding. The elevator doors whooshed open, and I stepped inside, hitting the "close" button immediately.

"Hey!" the lady cop shouted. "Hold the elevator!"

I raised my hand and blew them a kiss as the doors slid shut. Too slow, Joes. I heard the cop shout "Stop!" just before the elevator car started its speedy ascent.

The building was on the newer side, and the elevator was fast, but the ride up to the sixtieth floor seemed to take forever. I counted my pounding heartbeats, hoping the exercise might provide some sense of calm. It was one Dom used to make me do when my temper or frustration would get the better of me, and it always helped. Not this time. Though this time I thought giving in to my emotions might actually be beneficial, especially when it came to pleading with Mari.

On floor sixty, the elevator dinged and the doors slid open once more, revealing the medical-chic lobby. It was just past six in the morning, late enough for a receptionist to be sitting at the curved desk a dozen or so yards across the polished composite floor. She looked up as I stepped out of the elevator, and a second later, her arm moved.

"Security to reception *immediately*," she said in a voice that should have been too quiet for me to hear. If I were human. I'm not.

She watched me cross the lobby, my bootfalls echoing off the walls. I stopped a few yards from the reception desk, hands in my coat pockets. "My name is Kat Dubois. Tell Dr. Marie Jones I'm here," I said, using Mari's pseudonym. "She's looking for me."

The receptionist offered me an icy smile. "She isn't currently in her office."

I withdrew my hands from my pockets ever so slowly. "I'm sure you have a way to get ahold of her. All you have to do is let her know I'm here." I sniffed a laugh. "What could be the harm in that?"

I heard the sound of multiple pairs of boots pounding against the hard floor. Security was on its way. Dealing with them would be annoying, but hardly much of a hindrance. So long as I could convince the receptionist to get a message to Mari, the plan was still on track.

I backed away from the desk and lowered myself to my knees, raising my hands and lacing my fingers together behind my head. "Call her," I said just as a cadre of well-armed security guards emerged from the hallway to the right of the lobby.

The black-clad men and women were in the process of surrounding me when the elevator dinged and the doors opened once more.

"Seattle PD!" a man shouted. "Drop your weapons!"

The security personnel backed away from me but didn't

disarm.

"We'll take it from here," the female cop said. I could hear her striding across the lobby, one shoe squeaking with each step. She came to a stop behind me. "Hands behind your back, ma'am."

I did as ordered, lowering my arms and pressing my wrists together behind my back, my eyes locked with the receptionist's. I could just make out the sound of a phone ringing in her headset.

"Make it quick," Mari said through the earpiece, her voice faint but clear. "The helicopter's waiting."

I raised a single eyebrow. She was pulling out all the stops to find me. I felt the corners of my lips draw up even as cold steel ratcheted around my wrists. This would work.

"There's a woman here to see you. The police are about to take her away, but—"

"Is it Kat?" Mari asked. "Does she have a sword?"

The receptionist frowned. "She does, yes."

"Do not let them take her!" Mari all but shouted. "Do anything, Janelle—anything! I don't care if you have to lock the police officers in a closet yourself, do *not* let them take her. I'll be on the roof in ten minutes. I want Kat there, waiting for me."

"I understand," Janelle said, then pressed a button on the side of her headset and stood. "I'm sorry." She flashed that ice-queen smile at the officers. "But we actually need her."

"This woman is under arrest for carrying illegal weapons," the female cop said, wrapping the fingers of one hand around my arm and pulling me up to my feet.

"I'm so sorry," the receptionist said. She came around the end of the desk, her movements graceful. "That's our fault. We asked her to come in looking like a threat to test our security protocols. It was a drill." She held her hands out before her. "Perhaps a poorly thought-out drill, but nothing more." When her eyes slid over me, her cheek twitched, but her smile didn't falter one bit. I couldn't imagine why anyone had given this woman the job of receptionist; she was about as warm and welcoming as Neptune.

"Do you have documentation of this 'drill'?" the police-woman asked. "We can't release her on your word alone."

"Of course." The receptionist extended her arm to the side, gesturing toward the hallway to the right of the lobby. "If you'll both follow me, I can show you."

"Forbes," the cop said to her partner. "Stay here."

Her partner nodded.

The receptionist's chilly smile became razor sharp. She was none too pleased. "Perhaps your partner would like to oversee the remainder of the drill?"

When her stare landed on me, I winked at her. She was a clever one, this Janelle. An ice queen, perhaps, but a clever ice queen.

Janelle looked past me, focusing on one of the security guards. "I believe they were just about to escort the 'intruder' to the helipad on the roof—it's a transport scenario." She flashed the lady cop a gracious smile. "Of course, they won't actually be flying anywhere. It's just—we're on a bit of a tight schedule, and we'd like the drill to be completed before business hours."

"Fine," the officer said. She headed for the receptionist. "Let's see this documentation."

21

Walking up a stairwell with your hands cuffed behind your back is awkward as hell. You're hyperconscious of foot placement and you don't want to look up, because if you trip, you will fall on your face. Literally. And faces and cement stairs don't play well together. Not ever. So yeah, walking up four flights of stairs in the middle of a long train of mercenary security guards was plain torture. Especially because the guards weren't moving nearly fast enough for me.

The counter on Dom's life was ticking down, only I had no idea how much time he had left. Maybe days. Maybe hours. Maybe only minutes.

The seven guards tromping up the stairwell ahead of me passed through a metal fire door and onto a terraced portion of the multitiered skyscraper's roof, one of the guards standing with his back to the door to hold it open. Cold air tunneled in through the doorway, carrying with it misty raindrops and the thwomp-thwomp-thwomp of helicopter blades chopping through the morning fog. As soon as I stepped through the doorway, wind whipped my hair around, the rain making strands stick to my face. Supremely annoying when I couldn't do anything about it. Damn handcuffs.

A helicopter touched down on the helipad near the jutting-out corner of the terrace. A few seconds later, Mari jumped out. She appeared to be wearing the same bloodied and torn skirt and blouse from the previous day. At least she'd lost the tattered lab coat. She held her hair down as she jogged away from the helicopter, running in heels like it was no big deal.

Nik followed her out onto the helipad, his long, black leather coat flapping around his legs as he took lengthy strides to catch up to Mari. He ducked slightly, the helicopter blades slicing through the air over his head.

Seeing Nik whole and healthy eliminated one link in a whole chain of fear and dread. All Garth had been able to tell me was that Nik had been there when he'd blacked out. I felt a burst of appreciation for Nik as I realized he must've fought off the other Nejeret. He was likely the only reason Garth was still alive. Nik didn't pull punches, and it dawned on me that the Nejeret might already be dead. I supposed it all depended on when exactly Mari had arrived.

My eyes locked on Mari's, and I took a couple steps forward, putting a negligible distance between me and the line of guards behind me, and jerked my cuffed hands upwards behind my back. I gritted my teeth against the pain as my right shoulder slipped out of its socket, but I pushed through the pain, pulling my hands over my head. The discomfort of the temporary shoulder dislocation was sharp, but brief. A bargain price to have my hands in front of me. I rolled my shoulder, making sure everything had settled back where it belonged. The joint ached, but the pain would fade quickly as it healed.

The corner of Nik's mouth lifted, just for a second. The movement caught my eye, and our stares met. His pale blue gaze was burning with worry. For me, I realized. Damn it, but seeing his concern for me warmed my shriveled little heart.

"I'm fine," I mouthed, flashing him my palm with the marbled Eye of Horus.

His eyes widened, relief washing over his face, and a true

smirk twisted his lips. He winked, his expression going blank a moment later.

"I've been looking everywhere for you," Mari said, voice raised to compete with the sound of the helicopter behind her. "You should've come straight here." She waved Nik forward. "Why haven't you been answering your phone? What if it's already too late?"

"It's not," I said, uncurling my fingers and showing them both my palm. The Eye of Horus glimmered in the pale dawn light, iridescent and inky. I didn't bother telling her my phone had been collateral damage during my dip in the Sound. "I'm fine, but Dom's not."

I looked into her eyes, searching for the woman I'd worked with so closely all those years we'd hunted rogue Nejerets together. For the woman who'd been like a sister to me. I just hoped some fragment of her remained. "He's going to die if we don't stick his *ba* back into him, and soon. Mars, there's no reason for Dom to suffer any longer. Nik's here, and I'm sure he'll agree to work with you, just like you wanted."

My gaze flicked to Nik. He shrugged one shoulder, the movement barely perceptible.

"All you have to do is save Dom. You're the only one who can reunite his *ba* with his body." I reached for her hand, gripping it tightly with both of mine. "Please. You have to come to the hospital with me."

Mari blinked, and it seemed like that was all it took for her mind to catch up and process what I was saying. She nodded once and gave my hands a squeeze. "Of course I'll help. We can take the helicopter." She pulled her hand free of mine and turned, jogging back to the helipad. "Fire it up!" she shouted to the pilot, waving one hand over her head in mimicry of the helicopter's blades in motion.

I followed her. When I reached the helicopter, I raised my arms to grip the overhead handle with both hands and lifted my right boot. Half in the helicopter's cabin, I glanced over my shoulder.

Nik stood a dozen paces back, his phone in his hand and his face angled downward.

"Nik!" I yelled. "Let's go!"

He lifted his face to me, his expression stricken. Slowly, he shook his head. "Kat . . ."

I dropped back down to the helipad and made my way to him, heart thumping and ears filled with the sound of the helicopter blades chopping through the air combined with my rushing blood. I could no longer feel the roof under my boots or the wind and rain swirling around me. All I felt was dread.

"My mom . . ." His pale blue eyes locked with mine. "I didn't see it earlier—my phone was dead, but I charged it as we flew. I'm so sorry, Kat. We're too late."

I stared at him, heart a misshapen lump of lead. *Don't say it. Don't say it. Don't say it.*

"Dom's dead."

22

Dom's dead.

My head was shaking all on its own. "I don't understand." My voice sounded hollow, the vibrations echoing around inside my skull. I was empty. Nik's words didn't make any sense.

Dom's dead.

Nik rested a hand on my shoulder, his pale eyes filled with sorrow. With pity. With grief.

"But . . ." Awkwardly, I withdrew the *anti-At* orb from my jacket pocket. Through the barely translucent, obsidian-like material, I could see Dom's soul twisting and swirling lazily. "But he's right here." I showed the orb to Nik, unable to take my eyes off it. "This was the plan. I—I did everything right."

I shook my head again, my heart beating in rhythm with the helicopter's blades. "We all agreed. It was supposed to work. I was supposed to save him." I looked at Nik, not understanding why we weren't flying back to the hospital right now. "We all agreed . . ."

Nik pressed his lips together into a thin, flat line, letting me work through this impossible reality.

Dom's dead.

"This isn't supposed to happen," I said, steel bleeding into my voice. "This was *never* supposed to happen." I clenched my jaw, breathing deeply through my nose. "He didn't do anything wrong. He was just trying to find our people . . . trying to help, and . . ." My fingers curled around the orb containing all that was left of my best friend and mentor. Of my brother. I stuffed it back into my pocket, eyes narrowing to slits.

This was Mari's fault. She was the one who'd trapped Dom's *ba* in the *anti-At* orb in the first place. Without her, he'd have healed like a normal Nejeret. Without her, he'd still be alive.

"Kat . . ." Nik's hand on my shoulder transformed from comforting to a warning grip. "Not here," he said, shooting a sideways glance over his shoulder. Nearly a dozen Ouroboros security guards still stood back there in a line with the police officer.

"If not here, then where?" I asked, a glare not meant for him cutting through his reticence. "He's dead, Nik. Dom's dead, and I have to know why—now. Here."

Nik returned my glare with a hard, measuring stare. After several seconds, he nodded. "Get your answers. I'll keep them off your back." Vines of crystalline *At* burst out of Nik's hands, reaching the guards between one heartbeat and the next, wrapping around each man and woman, the cop included, holding them and their weapons immobile. They wouldn't be going anywhere until he released them.

At the same time, I spun around, facing Mari and drawing my sword in one smooth motion. My hands were still cuffed together, but it wasn't too much of a hindrance. It just meant I'd be limited to two-handed sword moves. Power moves. Fine with me.

Mari had just dropped down to the helipad. She took a backward step, her rear flush against the helicopter, and held her hands out to me in placation. "Kat—"

I stalked across the helipad toward her. "You killed him!" I yelled.

Confusion filled her jade eyes.

"Dom's dead," I told her, stopping just out of sword's reach.

Mari's lips parted, but she didn't say anything. She just shook her head.

"Why? Why did he die? For what?" I pointed my sword at her, the tip of the katana's blade mere inches from her throat. "Tell me!" I screamed.

She licked her lips. "He was never meant to die." Her eyelids fluttered, tears gathering on her long lashes. "I just wanted Nik—I *need* him. I truly didn't know we'd captured Dom until you told me, but once I knew, I saw it for the opportunity it was—a way to coerce you into bringing Nik to me. A way to get you to convince Nik to work with me. He'd do anything for you. But then everything went wrong. If you'd just stayed put." A tear broke free, gliding down her perfect, pale cheek. "If you'd waited by that container like you were supposed to . . ."

"Don't turn this around on me. You're the one who tore out Dom's *ba*."

She shook her head vehemently. "No, Kat—"

"*You're* the one who trapped it in *anti-At* . . . the one who dragged him into that container and left him there to suffer without his *ba*. For all I know, you're the one who beat the shit out of him in the first place."

She didn't deny it.

"Why?"

She licked her lips, hair flying in her face. "Like I said, I needed to get to Nik, and the only way to do it was through you. He'd do *anything* for you."

It was my turn to shake my head. She was delusional if she thought that.

"You were supposed to bring him to the container yard. It was supposed to be a trade—Dom's life for Nik's cooperation. I'd have saved Dom if you'd given me the chance. Just like I'm trying to save our people."

"Our people don't need saving," I spat back at her.

"Oh, please. What would you know?" Green fire burned in her eyes. "You've been living with your head in the sand for years. You have no idea what's been going on . . . what's coming."

I moved the tip of the sword a fraction of an inch closer to her, forcing her to lean backwards into the helicopter's cabin. "What are you talking about?"

"They *know*, Kat." Her stare was hard, challenging. "About us—about our people. Ouroboros has hard proof. If I didn't help them by luring in Nejeret test subjects to use as lab rats, they'd have gone public. They'd have exposed us."

"I don't—" I shook my head. "That doesn't make any sense. Why not come forward? The Senate—"

"Is in on it," she snapped, cutting me off. "Where do you think Ouroboros got the proof in the first place? And the Nejerets I've been collecting—have you even seen the list? They're all loyalists and supporters of Heru and my mom. The Senate cut a deal with Ouroboros." Her jade eyes narrowed. "I was one of the first of our people they trapped; I *let* them take me so I could get on the inside. I'm walking on a tightrope here. If I misstep . . . if I even breathe wrong . . ." Her hands balled into fists. "I've found a way to save our people, but I need more time."

I inched closer until Mercy's razor-sharp tip was flush with Mari's skin. "Explain."

Mari swallowed, and the movement caused the *At* blade to cut into her skin. A droplet of blood snaked down her neck, leaving behind a crimson trail. "They think I'm helping them create some sort of a wonder drug based on our unique physiology." She grinned, lips closed and eyes hard. "I *have* found a way to make humans live forever, but it has nothing to do with science and everything to do with souls."

My eyes narrowed. "What do you mean?"

"A Nejeret *ba*—it's like a starfish. If you tear off a piece, it grows back. And if you extract a large enough piece, it grows back *twice*. The only problem is, encasing those fragments in *anti-At* taints them, and they become inviable. They kill their new hosts, even as they transform them. That's why I need Nik. Don't you see, Kat?" The feverish light of fanaticism glowed in her eyes, turning her irises radioactive. "I haven't found a way to make humans live forever. I've found a way to turn them into Nejerets. And if I turn enough of them into *us*, it won't matter when they go public with their exposé. We won't have to fear their fear, because *they'll be us*."

Slowly, I shook my head. "You're insane."

Mari laughed, the sound too high and tight, and the tip of my sword cut deeper. "Maybe, but that doesn't change the fact that our people need me . . . or that *I* need Nik." Her eyes searched mine. "Let me prove to you that you can trust me. The bargain still stands—Dom for Nik." She held out her hand. "Give me the orb. I'll put Dom's *ba* in a new body. He'll look different, but he'll still be *him*." Her chin trembled. "Please, Kat. This is for the good of our people."

I stared at her for so long that the strain of not blinking in the face of all that wind made my eyes burn. "Fine," I said, sheathing Mercy, and reached into my pocket. Hesitating for only a moment, I offered the orb containing Dom's soul to Mari.

Her fingers closed around it.

"No." Nik's voice was harsh behind me.

I peered back at him out of the corner of my eye.

"If you let her do this, Kat, it'll be murder. The human—"

"Would've only lived for a few more decades," Mari said. "Now he could live for millennia."

"His human soul will die." Nik strode closer, bringing himself into my line of sight. "Dom has lived for hundreds of years already, and his *ba* will continue on . . . somewhere. But whatever human she stuffs him into—Dom's *ba* will overtake that person completely. This life is the only shot a human soul has. Who are you to take that away?"

I felt torn, paralyzed by indecision.

Nik glanced at my left forearm, where the list of names of my dead were etched in *At* ink, shielded by my leather sleeve. Nik couldn't see it, but this close, I had no doubt that he could sense it. "Do you really want to add another name? A human life . . . with such a fleeting, fragile soul. It'll be your first true murder. The first time you'll end someone's existence, absolutely and completely."

I shook my head slowly as his words sunk in, each a dagger twisting into my gut.

"If you think you're ready for that guilt, Kitty Kat, by all means . . ."

I bowed my head, my eyes drifting shut. Every single person I'd killed up until now had been a Nejeret—traitorous to some degree, but a Nejeret containing an immortal soul in the form of a *ba* all the same. Each of my victims had continued on in that other form after I'd ended their earthly life. I couldn't say the same would happen for the soul of any human Dom's *ba* took over. Just as I couldn't say the same for my mom. Much as I wanted to see Dom again, I couldn't do it. Not like this. I wouldn't be able to face him, knowing the price some poor human had paid in order for him to live again.

"I'm sorry," I told Dom, voice soft as I reached for the orb containing his everlasting soul.

"So am I," Mari said. As she spoke, my fingers passed through the orb's no-longer-solid surface. She reached up and behind her, pulling herself into the helicopter's cabin.

My eyes widened, locked on the place where the orb had been. The inky *anti-At* had evaporated, giving way to a shimmering silver mist that scattered in the wind. It was Dom's soul. And it was floating away.

Panic surged, making my heartbeat trip over itself as it sped up. "Nik!" I shouted. "Can you capture him?"

The helicopter's blades picked up speed, sending the silver mist this way and that, scattering it further and further.

"I'll try!" he yelled.

I glanced at Mari. She was watching us with sad eyes from the back of the helicopter as it lifted off. "I'm sorry," she mouthed, tears streaming down her cheeks.

I considered leaping off the edge of the building in an attempt to latch onto one of the helicopter's landing skids, but it would be suicide with the handcuffs still in place.

"He's too scattered!" Nik called, bubbles of crystalline *At* pocking the air above the roof like three-dimensional polka dots containing pieces of Dom's soul.

I stood on the empty helipad, watching the last remnants of Dom blow away like so much dust in the wind, my heart shattering. I'd failed him.

He was gone. Really gone.

23

"Can you call him back somehow?" Nik shouted to me. His hair was matted to his scalp, and his cheeks were high with color. He was pushing his *sheut* to the max, juggling all of those little bubbles of *At*, even while creating new ones to trap this or that little tendril of Dom's soul. He wasn't giving up.

His determination soaked into me, and I shed my suffocating cloak of surrender. "Call him back *how*?"

"I don't know. Maybe write his name or draw a picture of him? *Something*?"

"I don't have a pen or paper or—"

"You have skin!"

My eyes widened, and a moment later, I dropped to my knees. I drew a dainty needle dagger from the sheath sewn into my left sleeve and didn't hesitate to scrape the sharp tip across my wrist. The blade bit into my skin, the sharp sting no match for my resolve.

D—O—

"Is it working?" I yelled to Nik as I began the *M*. It was awkward with the handcuffs still on.

"I think so, but—"

Halfway through the *M*, I glanced up at him. He was maybe ten yards from me, halfway between the helipad and the cluster of restrained security guards. And between us, a glittering silver mist was gathering, condensing into a mystical fog. It was working. It was *really* working.

"Dom?" My chin trembled, and I let out a shaky laugh, tears streaming down my cheeks. Setting down the knife, I reached out with one hand. My fingers sifted through his ethereal form like he was no more substantial than the air. The essence of him—his soul—tangled around my fingers in thin, ghostly filaments. "Stay with me?" I asked. I begged. "Please."

But even as I spoke, the shimmering mist that was *him* thinned.

"Hurry, Nik! Before he's too far away again!"

The mist parted as Nik pushed through. He crouched before me, elbows on his knees, and squinted around. "I've surrounded all three of us by a dome of *At*, but Kat, I can't let you out without losing some of him in the process. Bits of his *ba* are clinging to you . . ."

I hunched over and renewed the efforts on my arm with the knife. Maybe if I could just finish writing his name, I could coax him into me. Then, I could carry him with me forever.

"Kat." Nik's fingers wrapped around my knife wrist. "Stop. You have to stop."

"No, I don't."

"It's time to let him go." Nik brought his hand to my face like he was going to make me look at him, but I slapped it away. "Even if I captured him in *At*, then what? Are you really willing to hold him prisoner like that? For how long?"

I screamed, slamming the knife down on the cement tile so hard that the thin steel blade snapped in two. I glared at Nik, eyes burning with fury caused by the truth in his words—a truth I wasn't ready to face. "I'll find a way to bring him back."

"Let him have peace."

"I can't," I said, eyes on fire with something else entirely.

Tears streamed down my cheeks. "Two days ago, I drew a picture of him, and he raised his head and looked at me and told me he was alive, and *it was him*, Nik. For a few seconds, it was really Dom in that picture. He looked me in the eye and told me to find him, and I promised him I would." I cleared my throat and leveled my voice. "I'm not giving up on him yet. I'll share my own body with him if I have to."

"You don't know what you're saying, Kitty Kat." Nik's voice held a fierce warning. "You have no idea what it's like to never be alone in your body." But he knew. He'd done it for thousands of years, sharing his body with the soul of the god, Re. He might've been alone in his skin now, but the haunting pain shadowing his eyes was enough to give me pause.

"But I promised him . . ."

The rising sun peeked over a nearby building, brilliant sunlight streaming in through the *At* surrounding us and setting Dom's *ba* aglow. Realization dawned just as suddenly.

In that drawing, it was *him*. With that single sketch, ink on paper, just for a blip of time, I'd captured Dom's soul—when it had still been inside him. Now, here his *ba* was, homeless. What if I gave it a home? Not another body, exactly, but something else. Something like the sketch, but better. Something to tide him over until I could figure out a way to give him a body that didn't include murdering a human.

"I think there's another way . . ." I fished my drowned phone from my coat pocket and set it on the helipad. "Do you mind?" I asked Nik, holding my cuffed wrists out to him.

Without a word, he touched the chain connecting the handcuffs. The metal turned opalescent one second as Nik transformed it into *At*, then seemed to evaporate the next, leaving my wrists naked of all but ink and blood.

"Thanks." I hunched over on my knees and drew the second needle dagger stowed in my other sleeve, holding it by the blade like it was a harmless pencil. With the tip of the blade, I started etching Dom's face into the phone's reflective surface.

Dom. I focused every ounce of brainpower on thinking about my half-brother. On remembering the way his dark eyes could pin me in place the same way, whether they were filled with disappointment or with pride. On remembering the way his severe features softened on those rare occasions that he smiled. On remembering how he would slick back his black, chin-length hair whenever he had something to say but was holding his tongue. On remembering how he listened. How he'd chosen to spend time training me when there were a million better things for him to be doing. On how he'd given a shit about me, even when I hadn't.

I wiped a raindrop off the phone's surface with the side of my hand. An electric charge seemed to pass through me and into the phone.

"Kat, look . . ."

I shushed Nik, adding shadows to Dom's face in the form of faintly etched lines. I wiped away another raindrop. "Do you mind?" I said, glancing at Nik, then up at the cloudy sky.

Except the sky was an iridescent color. Because it wasn't the sky, but Nik's dome of *At*. And the those weren't raindrops; they were tears. *My* tears. There was no wind or rain in here. No sound but our own.

It took me a moment to realize I could see the dome of *At* clearly, not through a shimmering, unearthly silver mist.

"Where'd Dom go?"

Nik's face was ghostly pale. "I'm pretty sure he's in there," he said, reaching out and tapping the side of the dead phone.

I stared at the image etched on the surface. At first I

thought it was a trick of the eye, but ever so slowly, I watched the image of Dom's face move. His lips parted. His mouth opened. And he let out a silent scream.

"He doesn't look too comfortable," Nik said dryly.

"I did it." I looked from the phone—from Dom—to Nik and back. "I really did it." I held up the phone like I was taking a selfie. "Can you hear me, Dom?"

Ever so slowly, the etched likeness of him shut his mouth. The rough copies of his eyes seemed to be seeking without seeing.

"I promise I'll make you more comfortable soon, and I swear to all the gods who've ever existed, I will make you whole again." I tucked him back into my pocket, then met Nik's eyes. "Don't tell anyone about this yet," I whispered. "I don't want them to get their hopes up."

Nik said nothing for long seconds, just looked at me with those pale, guarded eyes. Finally, he nodded. "I'll keep your secret," he said. "For now."

24

Nik and I burst out of the Columbia Center to the sidewalk on Fifth Avenue. My helmet was gone, likely stolen by some enterprising passerby, but the Ducati was still parked there, illegal as ever. I'd feared it would already have been towed. But, after everything, I'd only been in the building for *maybe* twenty minutes. I'd have bet a tow truck was already on its way. But it wasn't here yet.

"Can you ride?" I asked Nik as we sprinted to the bike.

He looked at me, *You're kidding, right?* in his eyes.

I snorted. "Good, because you're too tall to ride behind me." I handed him the key and waited for him to mount before kicking my leg over the seat behind him.

The Ducati Monster is not a bike designed with multiple riders in mind. Sure, it's got a narrow little extension behind the main portion of the saddle for a passenger and two tiny little kick-down pegs on either side, but the crunched-up position isn't comfortable for the passenger, and the rider has to deal with the annoyance of being top-heavy and having the passenger leaning on them, due to the passenger's raised seat. But damn, in all black with just a hint of candy-apple red, the bike is sexy as hell. And it can *move.* To say I loved my motorcycle was putting it lightly.

"And Nik, if you crash this bike . . ."

Nik kicked the bike to life like he owned it and, fingers

gripping the handlebars, waited for me to wrap my arms around his waist from behind before putting it in gear and turning the throttle. We'd never sat this close together before—not ever. I was pressed up against the back of him, our bodies touching from knees to shoulders. I'd ridden with other people a few times, but it had never felt this intimate.

"Relax," Nik said over his shoulder. "I know what I'm doing."

But the tension coiling through my body had nothing to do with the bike or his riding ability and everything to do with him. With his body, snug between my legs.

Once upon a time, a long, *long* time ago, Nik and I shared a kiss. It was back during his possessed-by-a-god days, and the god, Re, had flipped out almost the moment our lips touched. It had been a breaking point for Re, forcing him to wrest back control from his host. It had had the feel of a last-straw moment. A shattering of a pact between the two beings sharing his body.

We'd never talked about it, about any of it—the kiss, the explosion, Nik's increasingly tenuous relationship between himself and his now-former resident god. Considering Nik's arm's-length attitude, I doubted we ever would. But sitting there, my legs straddling his, I couldn't help but wonder *what if?*

Nik braked at a stop sign, placing his feet on the pavement on either side of the bike, and turned his head so he could see me. "Where to?" We were at a literal fork in the road—right would take us to the hospital, left back to my shop. But there was nothing left for us at the hospital. At least, nothing urgent.

"Back to the shop?" I said, resting my chin on Nik's shoulder. After the events at the Columbia Center, I had no doubt that the police would eventually find their way there, but I figured we had at least an hour or two. I was planning to head back to Bainbridge—finally—where I would give the Dom situation my full attention, but there were things I needed to grab from my place. Things I didn't want the cops or anyone else to find, my tarot cards and the *At* ink chief among them.

Plus, I stank. I reeked of mildew and seaweed, thanks to my dip in the waterway and the slow dry that had followed. The smell was strong enough that I couldn't ignore it; it had to be overwhelming to Nik. "I could really use a shower."

"You said it . . ." Nik turned the throttle, launching the bike forward before I could smack him.

We arrived at the shop less than ten minutes later, parking in the back alleyway, right near the shop's back door. It felt like weeks since I'd been home, though it had been less than a day. So much had happened. Too much. I didn't want to think about it all.

The shop would be opening in a couple hours, and I needed to be far from there when it did. I had to clean up and clear out—or clear out as much as I could as the place's owner. It was too risky to hang out there, and the cops paying me a visit was the least of my worries. Mari was a loose cannon, and I was a loose thread. I didn't know if anything she'd said was the truth, or if had all been a lie to ease her getaway. Would she come after Nik again? How badly did she need him? What kind of bargain might she try to strike next—either Nik helps her or she kills me? Lex? His mom? None of those were acceptable possibilities.

I unbuckled my sword's shoulder harness as I tromped up the stairs to the apartment ahead of Nik. I unlocked the door and shouldered it open, already shrugging out of my stinky leather coat. "I'll be quick," I told Nik as I crossed the living room to the kitchen. I set the coat and sword on the table, then pulled out a chair and sat with a groan, bending over to untie my combat boots. Salt had crusted into the laces, making the knots insanely stubborn.

"Looks like you had to go through a regeneration cycle," Nik said from just behind my chair.

I froze while untying my boot, peering at him out of the corner of my eye. I hadn't noticed him draw so close. He was looming over me, his gaze scrutinizing, eating a piece of cold pepperoni pizza.

I finished untying the right boot and moved on to the left. "Will you grab me a piece? Or just pull out the whole thing?"

His shadow moved away from me. "Mari wasn't sure how bad she got you with that knife." I heard the fridge open, then close, and Nik set a ziplock bag of cold pizza slices on the table near the edge. "Bad enough for you to look like you just escaped from a prison camp."

I tugged my left boot off. "Gee, thanks." I pulled off the other boot, then straightened and grabbed a piece of pizza. "So what happened to you, anyway? Garth barely survived . . ."

"But he did?" Nik pulled out the chair opposite mine. It wasn't a large table, so it didn't put him more than four feet from me. "I wasn't sure he would."

Chewing, I nodded. "He's in ICU at Harborview. I visited him while we were waiting for Dom—" The words caught in my throat. I took another bite of pizza, then set the half-eaten piece on the plastic bag and dug around in my coat until I found my phone. Dom's eyes were closed, but at least he was still there. *I'll fix this,* I promised him silently. I retrieved the piece of pizza. "Garth said a Nejeret attacked you guys and knocked him out, and when he came to, you were gone."

Nik nodded slowly, nibbling on pizza crust. "The fucker

jumped us. Hopped right off the overpass and landed on my
shoulders, knocking me out cold for a few seconds. I came to
my senses and managed to shove him off the cop before,
well . . ." Nik laughed under his breath. "Not soon enough. I'm
just glad the guy's alright."

I leveled a steady stare across the table on Nik. "And the
Nejeret—what happened to him?"

Nik met my eyes, then looked away, a wry grin on his face
as he shook his head. "I don't know. Mari showed up before I
could finish him. She would only agree to take me to you if I
let the little shit live." His pale eyes returned to mine, shining
unexpected emotion. He smirked, ruining the moment, and
said, "I couldn't let you fade into nonexistence, now could I,
Kitty Kat?"

I'd have been flattered that he cared if I didn't know that
he was even more attached to this world as it was now than
Mari was. If I were to be erased from the timeline, millennia of
Nik's life would be altered, thanks to the complicated tangle of
time travel. I'd never considered that the ramifications of my
life might be so far-reaching. But they were.

I looked at the Eye of Horus tattooed on my palm. Maybe
Nik and Mari would've returned in time, before the *anti-At* in-
fecting my body erased me completely, and maybe Mari
would've released Dom's *ba*, allowing it to return to his body.
Maybe Nik would've listened to Mari, agreed with her logic
about saving our people, and gone to work with her at Ouroboros of his own free will. Maybe. But maybe not. We'd never
know.

I pulled another slice of pizza from the Ziploc bag, then
tossed the bag across the table to Nik. "Do you think she's
right?"

Nik raised his eyebrows.

"Mari. Do you think she's doing the right thing?" I rolled my eyes. "Trying to 'save our people'?"

Nik took a big bite of pizza, inhaling and exhaling slowly through his nose while he chewed. The way his squared jaw worked, defining the contours of his face that much more, made him almost irresistible. Finally, he swallowed, then spoke. "I think Mari thinks she's doing the right thing."

"Nice non-answer."

Nik shrugged one shoulder.

"Do you think it would really be so bad . . ." . . . *if the world knew about us?* It sounded so ridiculous in my head that I shoved the thought away, shook my head, and stood. "Never mind." I didn't have the energy for what-ifs right now. I headed into the hallway. "I'm showering. I'll be out in a few."

"Yes," Nik said. "It would be so bad."

I paused, my back to him and a hand against the hallway wall. "But if they see that we're not evil . . ." *They* being the humans.

"It's never about good and evil, Kitty Kat. I've seen countless civilizations rise and fall, and in the end, it always comes down to two things—us versus them, and power."

"In this case, are we 'us' or 'them'?"

"We're 'them'—the other—and we have power. The humans can't help but want to take it from us. It's in their nature."

Hanging my head, I trudged into the bathroom. But I wasn't convinced he was right. I wasn't convinced the humans were our enemies—or that *we* were *theirs*. I wasn't convinced we couldn't all live together, peacefully, out in the open.

One day, maybe . . .

But not today. Today was for the enemy within. The Senate. Or the *shadow* Senate. We had to eliminate that threat before we could even think about a world filled with hand-holding and kumbayas.

After I no longer smelled like a dried-up seal carcass.

25

By the time I emerged from my bedroom, clean and in fresh jeans and a black tank top, Nik was gone. It hadn't even been ten minutes, but I wasn't surprised, exactly. At least, not by his absence. I hadn't really expected him to stick around, not when he'd been in the wind for years. But I was surprised by the disappointment I felt at finding the apartment empty. Specifically, empty of *him*.

As I stuffed clothes into a duffel bag, I wondered where he'd gone. Off to return to his lifestyle as a wandering nomad? Or was he joining up with Mari's mission to save the world, one human-turned-Nejeret at a time? My motions became jerkier and jerkier as I crammed only the essentials into the bag—underwear, socks, jeans, tank tops and T-shirts, a zip-up hoodie. The bastard could've at least said goodbye.

I hooked my arm through the bag's handles and carried it into the kitchen by my elbow. Setting it on the table, I added my sword, knives, and other weapons and gear, then zipped it up. A quick trip into the office and I carried out a sturdy leather messenger bag packed full of sketching supplies and cash from the safe, the red leather jacket I used to wear on hunts slung over my arm. It had been in the weapons closet, and I hadn't worn it in ages. Donning it was like stepping back in time.

I could feel myself becoming *her*, the girl-assassin I'd been desperate to become at the start and had, by the end, loathed being. As the jacket settled on my shoulders, hugging my back and fitting perfectly around my arms, I realized I would always be her—just like I would always be the girl my mom raised, and the woman I'd become during my years of self-inflicted isolation from my people. Whatever else happened to me, those three personas would always be a part of me.

Jacket on, I tucked my tarot deck into the front pocket, grabbed the last piece of pizza from the ziplock bag, and put it in my mouth, holding it by the crust with my teeth. I picked up both bags, settling the messenger bag across my body and hoisting the duffel onto one shoulder.

I headed downstairs as I chomped on the piece of pizza, dropping my duffel on the table in the back room and going into the shop to grab my tattoo machine, a handful of sealed needles, a couple bottles of black ink, and Nik's *At* ink. I placed everything in the padded carrying case I used for off-site jobs. The case looks a lot like an old-fashioned doctor's kit and was actually my mom's old apothecary case. She'd never been a fan of tattoos, but I doubted she'd have minded me using it, even for this.

I set the case down by my duffel bag on the table and stopped by the counter to scrawl a quick note to Kimi on a sticky note.

Kimi—

I have a family emergency and will be out of town for a while. I'm not sure how long. I'll call later today to check in, but please alert any clients I (or Nik) have this week. Thx!

—K

I stuck the note to the face of the register, where I knew Kimi couldn't miss it, then crouched down to retrieve the spare key to the upstairs apartment that I kept duct-taped to the underside of the counter in a tiny manila envelope. On the not-so-off chance that Mari or Ouroboros came after me here and ransacked the place, I didn't want them gaining easy access to my apartment. The door was reinforced and quadruple-locked, and I'd slowly renovated the windows and walls over the years, replacing and reinforcing for the highest security I could afford.

Someone knocked on the shop's glass door.

Fingers still searching the rough surface for the key, I peeked over the top of the counter. "Shit," I hissed, ducking back down immediately. The police had come sooner than I'd expected.

Two cops stood at the door, one peering in, hands to the glass over his eyes, the other leaning back, scoping out the storefront. I didn't recognize either of them from Garth's station or the ICU waiting room, so I assumed they weren't here to bring me news about Garth—not that I really thought I'd have warranted such a visit, but still. It was a possibility. But not the most likely one.

No, these cops were here because of what happened less than an hour ago downtown. Back at Ouroboros, Nik and I had left the male cop locked on the roof terrace with the Ouroboros guards, and we'd made it down to the bike without encountering his partner. It would've been a breeze for them to ID me—either by security cameras or by taking down the plates on my illegally parked motorcycle. However they'd done it, they'd tracked me back here. I'd expected as much, just not this quickly.

I stuck my whole head under the counter to find the damn

key and tore the damn thing free of the underside of the counter, then crawled into the backroom, sliding under the beaded curtain to avoid creating movement that would draw the officers' attention. The longest strings of beads ended not quite a foot off the ground, giving me just enough room to wiggle underneath.

The cops rapped on the door again. "Police! Open up!"

I grabbed my duffel bag and the carrying case and rushed down the short hallway to the back door. It led to the alley driveway, where some of the other shops and the single cafe on my block received deliveries. I fully intended to make a quick getaway on the Ducati, bags and all, then ditch it in some other neighborhood to catch a bus to the ferry. Reprehensible as the thought was, the bike was too recognizable to take with me for farther than a few miles.

I yanked open the door and sucked in a breath to let out a startled scream.

Nik's hand clapped over my mouth, and he stepped in through the doorway, shoving me back against the hallway wall. "You've got visitors," he said, his face inches from mine, and I nodded.

This close, I could see the whitish, almost iridescent flecks interspersed throughout his blue irises, giving them that eerie, pale hue. I'd never seen them so up close, and I wondered if the iridescence had grown over time, evidence of the increasing power of his *sheut*. He was the oldest of our subspecies, Nejerets with *sheuts*, and he'd had the most time to develop his otherworldly power, to hone his skills. Had his irises been bluer, once upon a time? One day, would the blue fade away completely?

Nik's hand fell away, and he took a step backward. His other hand held up a tray with two coffee cups, and a grease-stained paper bag lay on its side on the asphalt in the alley behind him. "Now might be a good time to make like a tree and get the fuck out of here."

Again, I nodded.

Nik backed through the doorway, doing a quick scan of either direction, and held out his hand. "Give me your bag."

There was no question that he meant the duffel, and I didn't argue. He was bigger and stronger, and me carrying so much would just slow us down. I dropped the bag to the floor and kicked it to him while I readjusted the messenger bag's strap on my shoulder.

Nik picked up the duffel bag, slinging the strap over his shoulder, then bent over to retrieve the discarded paper bag.

One whiff of sugary, fried dough told me it was filled with donuts. "You left to get breakfast?" Astonishment knocked me momentarily senseless.

Nik scoffed and waved me out into the alleyway. "Ticktock, Kitty Kat. I'd rather not have to break your ass out of jail. Let's go."

I didn't argue. A rush of giddiness surged through me as I followed him out through the doorway. We ran up the alley and hopped on the first bus we saw, not caring where it would take us.

To the University District, it turned out. Four stops later, we were off that bus and waiting at the main bus stop at the University of Washington on Fifteenth Avenue. In minutes, we'd be on our way to the ferry terminal downtown, and in hours we'd be stepping onto Bainbridge Island. There, I would be able to figure out some way to make Dom's afterlife more comfortable. *There*, Nik and I would be able to reconvene with our people—the non-traitorous ones—and figure out what the hell to do. Our world was a ticking time bomb crafted by our own people. Evidence of our species was out there, in human hands.

I didn't think it wasn't a matter of *if* the bomb would explode, but *when*. I just hoped we'd be ready.

26

I sat on the floor in my old room on the second floor of Heru's house in the Nejeret complex on Bainbridge Island, surrounded by my old things. Now, even more so than before, I felt the convergence of who I used to be and who I was now. I was at a crossroads. I could drop everything—my sword, my shop, my name—and go on the run, be a lonely woman on the lam. I'd be running from myself as much as from anything else. Or I could give in. Accept who and what I was, both to myself and to my Nejeret clan.

The desire to run was strong. After all, it was essentially what I'd been doing for the last three years—running from the past while staying put, anchored to it. Running was safe. It was simple. It was lonesome but devoid of the complications and utter devastation that come with strong bonds.

But as I etched Dom's full name, Dominic l'Aragne, into the wood frame of the standing mirror laid down on the floor before me, over and over, Lex's words in that hospital stairwell—her plea—reverberated within me. *Be the legacy she deserves.* I couldn't shake the nagging feeling that she was right, that my mom would be disappointed in the woman I'd become. Not the killer, but the recluse. The one who chose to hide from her past mistakes rather than learn from them.

I'd distanced myself from my people, from Dom, and now he was gone . . . or gone-*ish*. And just like when my mom died,

I was inundated with regret about time lost. Time *wasted*. I'd unwittingly thrown away the chance to see Dom a thousand more times, to share hundreds of philosophical conversations with him, to know him better. To let him know *me* better.

It's a funny thing, being a supposed immortal being. I'm only into my fourth decade, but even I have the deep-seeded belief that I and all of my Nejeret friends and family will be around forever. I'd been going through life the past few years thinking that someday, a good ways down the road, when I've got my shit together, I'd come back to them. But I'd been waiting until I'd become someone worthy of the love they're so willing to throw my way. I'd been waiting for a day that would never come.

I shook my head and started the thirteenth iteration of Dom's name around the mirror's wooden frame. I'd figured Dom and I would reunite someday, the dynamic duo, kicking ass and taking names side by side. And now that someday would never come. I was holding onto what little remained of him, my fingernails digging into his soul in a desperate attempt to regain what could've been. Possibilities that I'd thrown away so carelessly.

"I'll make this right," I told the phone sitting on the floor beside my knee.

Dom's etched eyes were open, his sharp, rough-hewn features arranged in a pattern that I thought might, just maybe, be curiosity. I was fairly sure he could hear me, though that etched image of him moved so slowly that any responses he gave may have just been coincidental movements. I blamed his hindered mobility on the medium. Etched glass was too permanent, too hard for his *ba* to manipulate. This time I'd used ink—Sharpie, to be exact. And I'd given him a full body, taking up the entire mirror when I drew him in painstaking detail, right down to his favorite loafers with the little leather tassel things. I'd always teased him about those.

There was a knock at the bedroom door.

"Yeah?" I called over my shoulder. I wasn't ready to share Dom with the others yet, not until I knew there was a way for us to communicate with him—for him to communicate with us. Not until I knew I wasn't torturing him by keeping him here. I wanted his permission, his blessing, before I let the others know just how desperate I was to hold onto him.

"It's me," Nik said. He turned the locked door handle. "Can I come in?"

"Sure." I didn't bother getting up to unlock the door. He could do it himself by magicking up a key out of thin air. "Lock it again, though," I said, once he was in the room. Lex, Heru, and the others were still on the west side of the Puget Sound, but there were plenty of other Nejerets who lived in the Heru compound and had keys to this house. Nobody could know about Dom until I was certain. Until I—*we*—were ready.

Nik locked the door, just like I requested, and his footsteps were quiet as he crossed the room to stand behind me. He whistled. "That's Dom, alright. Nicely done."

I finished the "e" in Dom's surname, then started carving the final rendition of his name around the wooden frame. "Thanks." I was quiet for a moment. "Nik . . . am I doing the right thing?"

Nik stepped over the mirror and sat in the cushy armchair by the window. "Honestly, Kitty Kat, I'm the last person you should be asking about right and wrong."

I frowned but continued carving.

"What would Dom say?"

"That's what I'm trying to find out," I grumbled.

Silence settled between us while I finished that final carving of Dom's name. My hand ached, and my fingers were cramping, but I pushed through. Finally, I sat back on my heels and set the wood-handled carving knife on the floor, trading it for my dead phone. I held up the phone so I could look at Dom face to face, my lips pursing in thought. My focus shifted from Dom's face to Nik's. "Any idea how to get him out of here and into the mirror?"

Nik shrugged. "You're the Ink Witch."

I scowled. "Don't call me that. I hate that nickname."

"You used to say that about 'Kitty Kat,'" Nik said with a smirk. "Maybe it'll grow on you."

"I hate that nickname, too," I lied.

Nik's smirk widened knowingly. "Of course you do."

Heat creeped up my neck and cheeks, and I bowed my head, letting my dark hair fall around my face, a curtain hiding the unexpected blush. "I still hate you," I told him.

"Of course you do," he repeated, his voice even more mocking than before.

I closed my eyes and took slow, deep breaths, focusing on Dom's dark, secretive eyes. In seconds the mental image replaced Nik's pale stare, and I felt myself become centered within. Nik had a tendency to make my thoughts and emotions flail wildly, while Dom had always been able to ground me. Maybe it was why I was so desperate to hang onto him.

"Touch."

My eyes snapped open, and I looked at Nik. "What did you say?"

Frowning, Nik shook his head. "Nothing." He was sitting on the edge of the chair, his elbows on his knees and his keen gaze locked on me, watching me do my magic. He was probably hoping to learn something, to understand, to figure out *how* I do what I do so he can train to do it himself. Everyone with a *sheut* could learn to do new things, train themselves to access more facets of their otherworldly powers . . . to some degree. I was still trying to master my own damn innate power. It was like trying to leash a kraken.

Eyebrows drawing together, I stared down at the phone. Dom returned my stare with so much intensity I had no doubt that he could truly see me.

"Touch . . . mirror . . ." There was no mistaking it this time—it was Dom's voice whispering through my mind.

"Did you hear that?" I asked Nik, eyes flicking his way.

Again, he shook his head.

I licked my lips and, hands shaking, lowered the phone to the mirror. I set it down on the drawn-on glass and held my breath.

Nothing happened.

For nearly a minute, I watched, waiting. But nothing happened. Dom just stared back at me from the phone's screen, blinking every ten or fifteen seconds.

"Maybe turn it over?" Nik suggested.

"Oh, right." I gently flipped the phone over so it was facedown against the mirror.

Almost immediately, silver poured into the mirror, billowing out below the surface like ink in water. Strands of it shot up from the mirror's surface, diving back down almost immediately as the silvery filaments coiled around the lines of the drawing until the ink from the permanent marker was no longer black, but solid, gleaming silver.

My hands covered my mouth, my eyes bulging. Tears streamed down my cheeks as I watched the impossible happen.

The now-silver drawing deepened, gaining shadow and depth, becoming three-dimensional right before my eyes. Dom seemed to gain weight even as he gained substance, and his feet fell away, as though drawn by some other-dimensional form of gravity, until he was standing on an unseen surface below, face upraised. He stared up at me through the mirror.

"Help me," I said to Nik, reaching for the mirror's edges. I gripped either side and lifted it a few inches off the ground, intending to stand it upright.

"Little sister—"

I dropped the mirror back to the floor, hands clutching my chest. Dom's voice had been clear as day in my mind. There was no mistaking it. I looked from Dom in the mirror to Nik and back. Dom's mouth was still moving, but his voice was gone.

Without hesitation, I pressed my palm against the frame of the mirror.

"Can you truly hear me?" Dom asked, his faint French accent more comforting than any hug had ever been.

"Yes," I said, chin trembling. Let's be real, my whole body was trembling. I nodded, my free hand covering my mouth. "Are you alright?"

Dom nodded sedately. *"I am well enough. Though this position is not the most comfortable . . ."*

"Oh, right." Once again, I gripped either side of the tall standing mirror and lifted it up off the ground. Nik helped, and we moved the armchair aside and arranged Dom in the corner of the room, where he would have a good view of the entire space.

"Thank you," Dom said. *"That is much better."*

Nik's eyes opened wide, and a moment later, his lips spread into a broad grin. "Welcome back."

Dom's dark eyes locked on Nik. *"Should I say the same to you?"*

Nik chuckled. "We'll see." He looked at me. "Let go for a

minute." The moment I did, the mirror and its frame were taken over by a sheet of *At*, spreading out like ice freezing over a lake. Within seconds, the entire mirror had been transformed into *At*. "Wouldn't want him to break," he said as he pulled his hand back.

Remotely, I could feel myself nodding, hear myself saying thank you. But I couldn't tear my eyes away from my half-brother's face.

"I'll give the two of you a minute," Nik said, backing away. Out of the corner of my eye, I watched him turn and leave the room, shutting the door on his way out.

I touched the mirror's unbreakable *At* frame with trembling fingertips so I could once again hear Dom's voice. "Dom, I—I'm so sorry . . . for everything. I tried so hard to save you, but I just wasn't good enough."

His silvery reflection clasped his fingers together, almost like he was preparing to pray. *"Answer me one thing, little sister, and all will be forgiven."*

"Anything," I said, meaning it with every fiber of my being.

"Are you done running?" His eyes, somehow just as dark and penetrating in silver as they'd been in flesh, bore into me. *"Are you back, for good?"*

I nodded vehemently. "Yes, Dom. I swear it. I'm back."

27

"And that's how you ended up in the phone," I told Dom, arching my back and stretching my arms over my head. I'd been sitting in front of the mirror—*his* mirror, now—legs folded under me and elbows on my knees, for nearly an hour. Dom's silvery non-reflection mirrored my position, if not the stretching.

I dropped my hands into my lap, flicking a few fingers at the mirror. "So what's it like in there, anyway?" I touched my fingertips to the base of the frame so I could hear his response.

"It is . . ." His eyes narrowed, and he looked around. *"It is strange. But also quite familiar."* His thin lips twisted into a wry smile. *"I'll let you know more once I've had a chance to explore."*

I nodded slowly.

"Kat . . . "

Uh-oh. I knew that tone—it was Dom's do-as-I-say tone. His I'm-disappointed-in-you tone. Especially when he actually used my name. Usually he called me "little sister." I held my breath.

"You need food," he said. *"And rest. You must allow your body to heal—another regeneration cycle, at least. You will continue to weaken until you do."*

"I know," I said, shaking my head. "I can't, though. Once Lex and Heru and the others get here with . . ." . . . *your body*. I cleared my throat, the words sticking, unspoken. "Once they get here, you need to tell them everything you can remember about Ouroboros, what they're up to, and where they kept you and the others. Now that we know some of the Senators are involved . . . I just have a feeling it's all going to blow up. I want to get those Nejerets—and those kids"—*especially* the kids—"somewhere safe before the Senate and Ouroboros figure out that we know what they're up to. We can't give them the chance to burn the evidence." It was a figure of speech, but in this case, I feared the reality would be far too literal. Those poor kids . . .

"Personally, I am more interested in why.*"*

I cocked my head to the side.

"Why did the Senate feed a human-owned and -run company the documentation proving our existence?" Dom said. *"Why are they funding Ouroboros? Why are they handing over Nejerets allied with Heru and Mei? Why have they deemed them the opposing faction?"*

I stared off into the background of the reflection, searching for answers where there were none. "And what's their endgame?" I said, adding to his list of questions.

It didn't make sense to me why any Senators would be involved in Ouroboros's plan to prolong human life indefinitely—it would only crowd the earth, especially if, unlike the females of our species, human women retained their ability to reproduce, even when relatively immortal. And why give them the proof of our existence, unless they *wanted* Ouroboros to share it with the world? It would create curiosity at first, closely followed by hostility, paranoia, and panic. Then, if Nik's fears proved true, all-out war.

"We can only speculate the reason behind their actions at this point," Dom said. *"And in your state, speculate poorly. Heru and the others have yet to return home, and there is little you can do without them. Rest, little sister."*

I rubbed a hand over my eyes. They felt gritty and dry, and my body ached with fatigue. I knew, in my bones, that Dom was right, but I wasn't ready to leave him just yet. Part of me feared he wouldn't be there when I woke up, like the magic would fade, and he would disappear from my life for good.

My mouth opened wide in a jaw-cracking yawn.

Dom stared at me through the mirror, his expression set.

"Fine," I said, giving in. "I'll take a damn nap." When I stood, I was surprised by how unsteady I felt. I touched the edge of the mirror so I could still hear him. "What will you do?"

Dom turned his head, looking over his shoulder. *"Why, explore my new realm, of course. I'm sensing that there's more to it than either of us might think."*

"Like what?" I asked, yawning once more.

"I am unsure, but there are . . ." He frowned. *"Sounds. And there are doors that do not exist on your side of the glass."* His frown faded. *"'There are more things in heaven and earth . . .'"*

It was my turn to frown. "Just don't get lost, alright? We need you." *I need you.*

Dom nodded. *"I won't go far."*

I held his reflected, silvery gaze for a moment, then nodded. Turning away from the tall mirror, I dragged my feet across the room to the bed and collapsed on it face-first. I was out within seconds.

"Just watch . . . one day, they'll know us." The rogue Nejeret, a slender guy with the innate sheut *power to camouflage himself like a chameleon, laughs bitterly.*

I'm standing over him, the tip of my sword perched on his chest, just over his heart.

"Killing me won't make one fucking difference." He coughs, blood spraying out of his mouth. I've worked him over pretty good already. He deserved it; he used those color-changing cells of his to rob several dozen banks, resulting in thirteen human deaths. "Just you watch—one day they'll know us. They'll see us for what we are: the cure sent to wipe the scourge that they are off the face of the earth. One day, they'll know us, and the next day, they'll die."

I put pressure on the sword, shoving the blade straight through his heart.

His whole body tenses, his eyes bulging. A moment later, he goes limp. "Self-righteous prick," I mumble, yanking the blade free.

"Tell me about it." Mari leans against the wall on the far side of the garage, cleaning her nails with the tip of an inky black nail file. "Maybe the world'll know about us one day"—her eyes met mine, almost highlighter green in the florescent lighting—"but only when we want them to. Only when we're ready . . ."

I sucked in a sharp breath and opened my eyes. Mari's words from my dream of a memory of something that happened sixteen years ago echoed through my mind.

. . . only when we want them to . . . only when we're ready . . .

Pushing myself up, I scooted to the edge of the bed, wiping the smear of drool from my cheek and chin with the back of my hand.

"Dom," I said, rushing across the room to the standing mirror. He wasn't there, at least, not that I could see. "Dom!" I pressed both hands against the frame on either side of the mirror and moved my head from side to side, searching for him in the murky reflection of the room.

"I am here," he said, coming into view. He smoothed back his hair and studied my face. *"What is it, little sister? Has something*

happened?"

I shook my head. "Not exactly, but . . ." I thought back to the dream. "What if the shadow Senate *wants* the info about us to leak out? What if they want the humans to learn about us? What if they *want* war?" My thoughts sped up, spinning around my mind like race cars around a track, faster and faster. "What if they want to wipe humans off the face of the earth?"

Dom's sharp features pinched. *"It would be suicide. Without a way to reproduce, eventually, our kind would die out as well. Besides, if that is their goal, why not simply release the information themselves?"*

I chewed on my thumbnail, seeking out a phantom hangnail. Nejerets' natural regenerative abilities effectively rendered us a doomed species, since it locked the females of our kind in a constant state of infertility. Our bodies rejected any fertilized eggs almost as soon as they implanted in our uterine walls. Without human women, we would die out. It would take a while, since violent deaths were pretty much the only way to kill us, but in time, we *would* go extinct. Whatever the shadow Senate's plans, they needed to keep some human women alive, specifically the ones who carried the latent recessive Nejeret genes.

"Oh my God." I lowered my hand, my mouth hanging open. "What if that's the whole point of funding the research—to create *some* immortal humans, a select, chosen few women who are Nejeret carriers? Maybe they want to give them prolonged lives, then use them as premier breeding stock. They could commoditize the right to reproduce . . . control who has access to the women. They would have absolute control over the future of our people."

"A truly terrifying thought."

I heard the distant sound of the front door opening downstairs, followed by several pairs of footsteps entering the house.

I looked at the bedroom door, then glanced at Dom. "They're back. Are you ready for them?"

He nodded.

"Nik!" I shouted in the general direction of the door. "Can you bring everyone up here?"

"On it," he said, tapping the door with his knuckles as he passed by.

I grabbed the throw off the back of the armchair and tossed it over the mirror. "Just for a sec," I whispered to Dom. "I want to prepare them first."

Less than a minute later, Nik pushed the door to my bedroom open and let the others file in ahead of him, first Lex, then Heru, then Neffe and Aset. They looked like hell, eyes red-rimmed and puffy and shoulders slumped. Nik followed them in, crossing the room to sit in the armchair.

"Nik tells us you have news," Heru said, his voice weary. He sidestepped closer to Lex and curled an arm around her waist. She leaned her cheek on his shoulder, letting out a heavy sigh.

"I know you all must think I failed, but I didn't." I took a step toward them, wringing my hands. "I found Mari . . . and she released Dom's *ba*."

Lex's head lifted, and her listless gaze wandered my way.

"It was too late," I said. "He was already—*his body* was already dead." I took a deep breath. "But we managed to recapture his *ba*."

Aset looked at her son.

Nik raised his hands in front of himself. "Not me," he said, shaking his head. "This soul capture was all Kat's doing."

All five sets of eyes fixed on me, curiosity muting the grief, just a little.

"I, um, well . . ." I cleared my throat and took a couple

small backward steps, moving closer to the covered mirror. "He's not gone—not dead, exactly." I reached out my right hand and pinched the fuzzy blanket. "He's right here." With one quick tug, the blanket slid off the mirror and fell to the floor.

Dom, the only clear thing in the murky reflection, lifted one hand and waved.

All four newcomers gasped. Neffe and Aset covered their mouths with their hands, and Lex took a couple steps forward, hand outstretched toward the mirror. Heru simply stood where he was and stared, golden eyes glassy.

"It's really him?" Lex asked, slowly moving closer.

"It is," I assured her.

"Can I talk to him? Can he hear me?"

I nodded. "He can hear you now, but you have to be touching the mirror to hear him."

She rushed forward, pressing her palm against the mirror. "Dom?"

A gentle smiled curved his lips and he raised his hand, pressing it against the other side of the mirror's surface. His lips moved, but lipreading was a skill I didn't have.

Lex rested her forehead against the mirror, shoulders shaking as soft sobs tumbled free.

Not a moment later, Heru was behind her. He settled an arm around her shoulders, the other on the mirror beside hers. "Welcome back, my old friend."

28

"So you can't say for sure where the warehouse was?" Heru paced across my old room, from the hallway door to the wardrobe and back. He'd been at it for at least an hour now, mobility seeming to help him process the information Dom relayed through me.

For the past hour or so, Dom had been explaining what had happened to him—how he'd been captured in a trap that resulted in the release of a knockout gas and what Ouroboros had done to him and the others while he was in their hands. Or rather, in their holding cells. According to Dom, the captive Nejerets were divided into two subject groups—those who were abused and brought to the brink of death, then allowed to regenerate, and those who'd had their *bas* extracted and *then* were abused and brought to the brink of death. Dom had been in the latter group.

He wasn't sure how the *ba*-extraction worked, science-wise, only that he'd been strapped down in a chair and that electricity had coursed through his body for what felt like an eternity. Once his soul was removed from his body, he had a brief moment of what felt like astral projection before he was encased in absolute darkness—the *anti-At* sphere closing in around him, we all assumed. His *ba* had been returned to his body several times during his several-week stay in the warehouse laboratory, allowing him to heal, but as a result, his moments of consciousness and lucidity were few and far between.

"I could hear the roar of the freeway, the frequent rumble of a foghorn in the distance, and, on occasion, the sound of a large crowd cheering— those are the only identifying sounds I can recall," Dom said, and I repeated his words to the others. Lex was sitting on the floor near me, Nik in the armchair in the corner, and Aset and Neffe on the foot of the bed. "Sounds like SoDo to me," I added. Not only was the industrial area packed with warehouses *and* near I-5 and the water, but it was also the location of Seattle's two professional sports stadiums—Safeco and Century Link Fields, where the Mariners and Seahawks played, respectively.

Heru nodded. "I agree, but there are hundreds of warehouses there, and I highly doubt Ouroboros would be reckless enough to leave any kind of paper trail linking them to their illicit research branch. We need more information."

"Mari," Dom said, voicing the option I was unwilling to suggest. *"She was there each time my ba was extracted. If you can find her, I am certain you could convince her to tell you the exact location."*

"We can't trust her," I told him. "She lied to me about knowing you were even there—said she didn't know until I told her. She's clearly got her own agenda. She's fanatical about 'saving our people.' It's the most important thing in the world to her."

"Is it truly?" He stared at me with those dark eyes. *"Is there not anything else you can think of that might be of paramount importance to her? Perhaps a person . . . ?"*

"Well, yeah—her mom, but . . ."

"Might Mari's priorities shift if she were to find out that her mother is just another test subject?"

My eyes widened. "Are you saying Ouroboros has Mei? That they're experimenting on her—*torturing* her?"

Dom shrugged. *"Truly, I do not know what they are doing with her, only that they have her. I watched them bring her in a few days ago during one of my recovery periods. They took her to a separate wing of holding cells."*

"Mari'd never allow that," I said.

"Then she must not know."

I shook my head. "But that doesn't make sense. Mei could just shift out of there." It was her innate *sheut* gift, along with a number of others she'd attained proficiency in through years of rigorous dedication and training. She was old, centuries beyond me in understanding and developing her *sheut*. I was still figuring out how my own innate powers worked. But her . . . I couldn't imagine anyone, especially not humans, figuring out a way to contain her.

"My holding cell was surrounded by an electromagnetic field that would keep those like Mei and Heru from being able to locate us—Mari explained it to me herself. It seems logical to me that the same field used to keep Mei out could be used to keep her in."

"Oh, shit . . ."

"Care to share?" Heru said, his tone bland. He'd finally stopped moving and was standing in the center of the room, staring at me.

I returned his stare. "How long since anyone's talked to Mei?"

Heru looked at his sister, who immediately pulled out a sleek cell phone and started tapping the screen. "You believe Ouroboros has captured her?" he asked, returning his attention to me.

I nodded. "Dom saw them bring her in." I relayed what he'd said about the electromagnetic field, then added, "If we tell Mari, she'll flip out." I shifted my legs so I was kneeling instead of sitting on the floor. My heart rate picked up, and I rubbed slightly sweaty palms on my jeans. "She'll abandon her 'save our people' crusade in a heartbeat and tear that place apart to get to Mei." I licked my lips and inhaled deeply. "If we tell her about this, she'll have no reason not to share the location."

Heru crossed his arms over his chest. "But what incentive will she have to help us? What's to stop her from simply going in there and breaking Mei out, and leaving us sitting on our thumbs?"

"Nothing." In all likelihood, I thought that was exactly what she would do. "But, her going in and breaking out Mei brings down all of the barriers. She'll disable all security measures in the process. And this is the only way I can see that she *might* tell us the location." I stared at each of them for a moment, settling on Heru's intense, golden eyes. "Back on that roof, she agreed to help Dom. She was going to come to the hospital and release his *ba*. She was going to help us save him." I had to believe that part hadn't been a lie. "She's not a bad person. Misguided, maybe, but not *bad*."

Heru rubbed his jaw with one hand.

"We can't wait to come up with something better," I persisted. "The shadow Senate will know that *we* know by now, thanks to our little show on the roof. Don't you think they'll try to cover their tracks by destroying all of the evidence—including the people?" I took a deep breath and barreled onward. "There are kids there, too, Heru. *Children* who didn't do anything wrong besides being unlucky enough to be homeless. They don't deserve this." My fingers gripped my jeans. "Besides, what's the worst that can happen? She leaves chaos in her wake? Ouroboros will send in extra security once they realize she's broken Mei out. You own companies that have satellites, don't you? If we have to, can't we just use them to monitor the whole Industrial District? Their own people will lead us right to the warehouse where they're holding ours."

Lex stood gracefully and approached her husband. She placed her hand on Heru's arm and looked up into his face. "She's right. You can see that, can't you?"

Heru's stare shifted from Lex to the mirror. Out of the corner of my eye, I saw Dom nod once. "Alright," Heru said. He looked at me. "Make the call."

I glanced at the scratched-up phone lying discarded on the floor. Her text from the previous day was the only place I had her number, and thanks to my dip in the sound, the phone would never turn on again. I bit my lower lip. Banging my head against the wall would be about as effective as this whole plan, because none of us had her damn phone number.

"Here," Nik said, fishing his phone from his pocket. He tossed it to me.

I raised an eyebrow.

"Her number's in there," he said, pointing to the phone in my hand with his chin. "She gave me her card . . . you know, because I 'agreed' to work with her."

A slow grin spread across my face. "Maybe I don't quite hate you."

Nik snorted. "Don't get soft on me now." His lips twisted into a sly smirk. "I'll blush."

I didn't know how to respond to that, so I stuck out my tongue. What can I say? I'm forever eighteen, with all the hormones and maturity that come with that oh-so-special age.

A slight tremor ran through my hands as I searched Nik's contacts for Mari's name. He had an enormous phone book, filled mostly with entries using distinctly female names. I ignored that little tidbit—for the most part—and found Mari's name. I pulled up her contact profile, tapped the call button, and brought the phone up to my ear.

She answered during the second ring. "Hello, Nikolas."

I responded without thinking. "His full name is Nekure, not Nikolas, numb-nuts."

"Kat?" From the way Mari said my name, she sounded wary.

"The one and only."

"You sound . . . chipper."

I sneered. "You know, I *feel* chipper."

"Really?"

"I just can't help but feel all tingly inside when I know something you don't know."

"Kat," Heru's voice held a warning, his eyes a dark promise.

I held up a finger, silencing him. I knew Mari better than him; I knew just how to play her like a concert pianist.

"And what might that be?" Mari asked over the phone.

"How about we trade—I'll tell you what *I* know, if you tell me where the warehouse containing your secret, evil lab is?"

"It's not my lab," she said blandly.

"Semantics," I said. "How about this—I'll go first. You don't have to tell me the location right away. You don't even have to tell me over the phone. You can text it to me, for all I care. But just remember one thing—you already owe me a debt for Dom's death. Now you'll be doubly indebted to me, and I'm not feeling too happy about you right now. The next time I see you, my sword might just slip out of my scabbard and accidentally pierce your heart. And trust me when I say I *will* see you again."

Mari was quiet for a few seconds. "Fine," she said. "I'll bite. Share."

I looked straight into Heru's eyes as I spoke. "Ouroboros has Mei, Mari. They have your mom."

Another few seconds of silence, just the sound of her breathing on the other side of the line. And then the line went dead.

Got her.

I lowered the phone, setting it on the floor by my knee.

Heru stalked toward me and crouched down, bringing his face to my level. Damn, but it was hard to look into those glorious black-rimmed gold eyes when he was so close and so very pissed off. "You're reckless," he said, his voice cold and controlled. And terrifying.

I leaned back a few inches. I couldn't help it.

"You've always been reckless," he continued. "If that causes our people their lives . . ."

Lex touched his shoulder with gentle fingertips, like doing so might help tame his rabid inner beast.

The phone buzzed, and I risked a glance downward. One new message. From Mari.

I opened it with a tap of my thumb. Straight-faced, I held the phone up for Heru to see. "If I'm not mistaken, that's an address." I suppressed a grin. "In SoDo."

29

8:57 PM
All bas have been released and returned to their respective bodies, security systems are disarmed, and personal are detained. Do what you want with this place . . . burn the whole damn warehouse to the ground if you want. I don't care.

8:58 PM
Just don't come looking for me. Don't look for my mom. You won't find us.

8:58 PM
This makes us even.

Mari's texts had come in quick succession while we were navigating the streets of SoDo. I'd smiled to myself after reading them. She'd always been reactionary. Once she cooled down and her more calculating, logical side took over, she would come to me, icy anger a frigid torch burning within her. Vengeance was a dish best served cold, in her case. And she made good chilled vengeance. The best, in fact.

We kept our rescue party small—Heru, Lex, Aset, Neffe,

Nik, and me. We were the only people outside of the shadow Senate fully aware of the situation. This core group was the trusted few, for now. Once the rescue mission was over and the warehouse lab was destroyed, we could start incorporating others into our circle—especially those we'd rescued—but for now, we were operating small, lips zipped. Loose lips and sinking ships, and all that . . .

Once we knew where to attack, getting people and the kids out was easy enough—knocking out anything electronic is simple when you have nearly unlimited funds and resources, which Heru does. It's good to be an ancient god of time—an 'old one,' as the more ancient of our kind were called. It helped that Mari had already swept through the place, disabling all of the alarm systems and security cameras and locking the few evening employees in holding cells that had apparently been empty.

We arrived just minutes after her texts, unleashing a localized electromagnetic pulse generator that would wipe out everything for as long as it remained on, giving us enough time to get in, release all of the captured Nejerets and kids, and get out. We rushed the former captives out to the three buses we'd rented to transport them back to the Heru compound on Bainbridge. We weren't sure what had been done to the kids. They didn't appear to be roughed up, but some seemed ill, and others were out cold. Neffe and Aset were determined to use every cell of their scientific brains to figure out what Ouroboros had done to them.

Not everyone could walk. Some of the Nejerets were unconscious, having slipped into regenerative comas as soon as Mari reunited their *bas* with their bodies. Those relative few were carried out, one by one, by Nik and Heru while Neffe, Aset, and Lex remained with those already loaded onto the buses, waiting to drive them to the ferry as soon as everyone was out. Reinforcements would arrive soon—Ouroboros had probably dispatched them as soon as Mari disabled all of the security systems—so we had to move as quickly as possible.

I remained within the heart of the lightless laboratory, keeping watch on the new captives while Nik and Heru ushered the wounded out. I paced from one end of the large, sterile room to the other, following the line of glass viewing panes giving me a window into the cells. There were eight cells in this portion of the warehouse, each holding two or three people— seven scientists and nine security guards.

"You can't hold us in here!" one of the scientists shouted, pounding a fist against the thick, tempered glass of the third cell from the end. "We were just doing our jobs!"

I rolled my eyes, blowing him a kiss as I passed the viewing window to his cell. He shared it with two other scientists—one male and one female. All three looked too pale, like they hadn't seen the sun in weeks. Then again, this was Seattle. None of us had seen the sun in weeks.

The rest of the room was filled with long, freestanding counters laden with high-tech and top-of-the-line equipment, all white or black or silver or glass. I didn't know what any of it was for, beyond the microscopes, but it didn't really matter. That was more Neffe's thing.

I watched Nik's back as he carried the last unconscious Nejeret out of the lab. Heru had left just a moment earlier, meaning I had a moment alone with the Ouroboros personnel.

Finally. This was why I'd volunteered to stand guard. This was what I'd been waiting for.

I stopped at the far end of the lab and reached into my coat pocket, pulling out a vintage silver compact mirror. It had been my mom's, and her mother's before her. I opened the compact, revealing the mirror that wasn't a mirror. DOMINIC

L'ARAGNE was etched around the outer edge of the glass in tiny, precise letters, and his silvery visage stared out at me, eyes squinting. My fingers trembled under the force of my adrenaline. I was starving for vengeance.

"Can you see?" I asked Dom, voice tight with the excitement of a potential righteous kill. "Or is it too dark?" There were no lights on in the warehouse, thanks to the steadily pulsing electromagnetic field generator we'd set up in the center of the cavernous building, but it wasn't too dim for keen Nejeret eyesight to see clearly enough.

"I cannot see much," Dom said, *"but I do not require sight to identify the one who tore out my soul."*

"Those people aren't even human!" the loudmouthed asshat scientist yelled. "They're not protected by any human rights laws!"

I quirked an eyebrow and started toward the third holding cell, picking up on Dom's meaning. He didn't need to see the guy who'd helped tear out his soul, because he could hear him, loud and clear. My bloodlust spiked, and my heartbeat quickened.

"We're well within our rights to do whatever the hell we want with them!"

"This one?" I asked Dom, stopping in front of the viewing window.

Dom nodded once. *"His is a voice I shall never forget."*

"Alright." I closed the compact and tucked Dom back into my pocket, then fixed my eyes on the irate scientist within. I cocked my head to the side, eyes scouring the lines of his face, memorizing his features. Fury lit my blood on fire when I looked at him.

His eyes searched what had to be absolute darkness from his perspective, looking for me.

"What's your name?" I asked.

"Dr. Bergman," he said, puffing up under his lab coat.

"Got a first name?"

He crossed his arms over his chest. "Eric."

I flashed him a humorless grin, not that he could see it. "Well, Dr. Eric Bergman, today's your lucky day. I'm going to let you out of that cell. You, and only you."

His eyes narrowed. "Why?"

"I need someone to send a message to your bosses. You're the most outspoken, so . . ." I nodded to the door, then re-membered that he couldn't see the motion. "Step on over to the door." When he didn't move, I added, "You want to get out of there, don't you? Isn't that what you've been going on about for the past ten minutes?"

After a few more seconds, he moved to the door. I un-locked it, and he took a cautious step out into the lab. A mo-ment later, he lunged to the side, attempting to make a run for it.

I grabbed the back collar of his lab coat and he jerked to a stop, falling back onto his ass. With my free hand, I pulled the door to the holding cell shut, then focused all of my attention on Dr. Dumbass.

"You, Dr. Eric Bergman, made a very big mistake," I said, taking hold of his thick mop of hair and pulling him up to a kneeling position.

He sucked in halting breaths. "I—I'm sorry. Your mes-sage—I'll pass it on. J—just tell me what it is."

I let out a bitter laugh, reaching into my back pocket with my free hand to retrieve a Sharpie. I pulled the cap off with my teeth and spit it to the side. "My brother's name is Dominic l'Aragne. He's one of the non-humans you so blithely experi-mented on." I leaned forward until my face was mere inches from his. I was breathing hard, impassioned by my rage. "I'm telling you this so you'll understand that what happens next is a result of your own actions. You made a choice. You chose wrong. You tore out my brother's soul, tortured him, and now he's dead." I glared at the man—the human—in disgust. He didn't deserve his soul. "It's time for the reckoning."

I pulled back a few inches and brought the Sharpie to his forehead, where I started to write out a single word in big, bold letters.

B—

His sweat blurred the lines of my letters, permanent ink and all, but it didn't matter. I was finally getting a grip on my *sheut*'s innate power. I was finally starting to understand it.

U—

Where my magic was concerned, intent was paramount, and conviction was key. There was nothing shoddy or shaky about my intent or my conviction now. The hunger for revenge was all-consuming. Dom's death would be answered for.

R—

I didn't even care that he was human, or that killing him would destroy his soul. That his would be the first life I truly ended, body and soul. He deserved an eternity of agony, but I'd settle for a few minutes instead. I wanted this man to burn with the fires of a thousand hells.

And burn he did.

As I finished writing the word "BURN" on his forehead, the ink started to sizzle.

Dr. Eric Bergman whimpered . . . then gasped . . . then screamed. The black letters pulsated, brilliant orange glowing around the edges. A moment later, actual flames burst out of his forehead. They engulfed his entire head, spreading down his body and up my arm. I gritted my teeth as my skin burned, blistered, and melted right along with his.

I threw him backwards before the flames could travel past my elbow. I didn't want to singe my hair, after all. My skin would heal in a matter of days, but my hair would take years to grow back.

Dr. Eric Bergman was still screaming when the lights came back on. Someone must've turned off the EMP generator. It was time to go. Bergman writhed on the ground, rolling and flopping around. I had no doubt that the pain was unbearable, that it had already driven him mad. And yet, there was no way it even came close to the hours and hours of pain and torture this man and his team had inflicted on Dom. Pity wasn't even a fleeting thought. This was justice.

Holding my arm away from my body, I walked to the nearest sink and turned on the water, moving my arm back and forth and twisting it around until all of the flames were out. Once I was fire-free, I strode away from the burning man still writhing on the floor.

Nik stood silhouetted in the doorway at the far end of the lab, shoulder leaned against the doorframe, watching.

I paused, just for a moment. I hadn't known he was there.

A moment later, I turned my head and looked at the scientists and security guards still in their cells. "I'm holding your bosses just as responsible as Dr. Bergman there," I told them. Every single one of them stood at their viewing windows, varying degrees of horror painted across their faces as they watched their colleague burn. "Feel free to let them know." I started to walk away. "And tell them I'm coming for them."

"But—"

I stopped at the last cell's viewing window.

Two of the cell's occupants slunk back into the shadows, but a lone female security guard stood her ground. "Who are you?" she asked.

"Me? I'm Kat Dubois." I turned away from her and continued on toward the doorway. Toward Nik. The ghost of a smile touched my lips. "I'm the Ink Witch."

30

"You're sure you can handle running this place while I'm gone?" I asked Kimi. It was evening, and the shop was closed.

From the opposite side of the counter, she shrugged. "I've been working for you since you first opened. If I can't run this place by now, I've got no business getting my MBA."

"Fair enough," I said with a nod. I bent my knees to pick up an oversized duffel bag off the floor. I'd stuffed nearly every piece of clothing I actually wore into the bag, along with my backup boots and a few other odds and ends from upstairs. "I'll check in at least once a week, but don't hesitate to call if you have any questions."

"You got it, boss," she said. "Any idea how long you'll be gone?"

I shook my head. "But I'll let you know as soon as I know." I was returning to Bainbridge indefinitely. It was past time for me to get over my shit and rejoin my clan.

The bell over the door jingled, and we both turned our heads to watch six people stream into the shop—Heru and Nik, closely followed by two unfamiliar Nejerets, one male, one female, and *him*. The bartender from the Goose smirked when his eyes locked with mine. The five newcomers lined up, Nik and Aset on either end, Heru a few steps ahead.

"Kimi," I said without taking my eyes off the Nejerets. "Why don't you take off. I'll finish closing up tonight."

"But—"

"Kimi." I looked at her, and whatever she saw in my eyes caused the blood to drain from her face. "Go, now. I'll call you tomorrow."

She nodded, licked her lips, and backed away, rushing through the beaded curtain. A few seconds later, I heard the back door open, then shut. Kimi was gone.

I refocused on Heru. "To what do I owe this honor, oh chieftain, my chieftain?"

"Katarina Dubois," Heru said, his voice bland, "the Senate has issued a detainment order for you. You're charged with being in league with the rogue Nejerets, Mari and Mei. Your rebellious and irresponsible actions have put Nejeretkind at risk, and such behavior cannot go unpunished." His lips twitched.

I, myself, was having a hard time keeping a straight face. I'd known something like this would be coming, eventually. I was the only one who identified herself at the warehouse the previous night, making myself the easiest target for retribution. We'd lit the match with our siege on the Ouroboros warehouse; it was time to start the fire.

"I advise that you submit to the Senate's authority and offer yourself into their just and capable hands," Heru continued. As leader of this territory, it was his right to come after me himself, though I wasn't surprised the Senate sent others with him to make sure he followed through. "If you do not submit, you will be detained using force."

Nik shook his head, almost imperceptibly.

I stared at him for a moment, then returned my focus to Heru. "You know," I said, "I'm just not feeling it today. Can you come back tomorrow?"

This time, when Heru's lips twitched, he allowed a hint of

a smile to break free, just for a moment. His expression went blank, and he turned on his heel to face the other Nejerets. "She chose to resist. There was a struggle."

"Was?" the bartender said, alarm flashing in his eyes.

Not a second later, crystalline *At* vines slithered across the floor, originating at Nik and wrapping around the ankles of the bartender and the two unfamiliar Nejerets. The vines climbed up their legs, winding around and around, until they were restrained up to their shoulders and their struggles were limited to the twisting of their heads from side to side.

"Fugitive's choice," Heru said. "Which to release as a messenger, which to keep for questioning . . ." He grinned viciously. "And which to *be* the message." There was no doubt in my mind what form that message would take. I was well versed in this form of communication.

I stared at Heru, unblinking, totally caught off guard. It was like a twisted version of marry-fuck-kill. "You're going to start a war," I told him.

"Not a war," he said, his grin fading. "A revolution."

"I—I don't—"

"Choose, Kat, or I'll choose for you."

I didn't even have to think about it, and I didn't bother voicing my choice. I simply drew the combat knife tucked into my boot sheath, strode up to the Nejeret who'd been posing as a bartender to spy on me, and held the blade flush under his jaw.

He swallowed reflexively.

"This is for Garth," I hissed, slicing the blade across his neck. I took a step backward to avoid the waterfall of blood that cascaded down his front and waited until his body went limp to turn away from him. I locked eyes with Heru. "I don't give two shits what you do with the others."

"Very well." His focus shifted beyond me, and he addressed the two remaining Senate Nejerets. "I'm declaring martial law." He looked at the woman. "Gaia, be so kind as to inform the Senate that my first act as Governor General is to pardon Katarina Dubois." As he spoke, the *At* vines restraining her uncoiled from around her body.

"You might want to go now," Nik said to the unfamiliar woman. The bell over the door jingled a moment later as she made a quick exit.

I watched the slowly expanding pool of crimson on the floor—it was going to be a pain in the ass to clean up—then sighed. In hindsight, maybe I should've just broken his neck, even if slicing it open had been more satisfying in the moment.

"How'd you know he was the one who attacked us?" Nik asked.

I met his eyes, but I could only handle looking at him for a second. I lowered my gaze to the puddle of blood on the floor. "I just did."

"Come on," Heru said, patting my shoulder. "Let's get this cleaned up. There's much to do, but little time. The sooner you're gone, the better."

"Gone?" I twisted around to look at him, brow furrowed. "Gone *where*?" Because the way he'd said *gone* sure as hell didn't sound like he was talking about our clan home on Bainbridge Island.

His golden stare was hard, commanding. "Underground."

About The Author

Lindsey Fairleigh lives her life with one foot in a book--as long as that book transports her to a magical world or bends the rules of science. Her novels, from post-apocalyptic to time travel and historical fantasy, always offer up a hearty dose of unreality, along with plenty of adventure and romance. When she's not working on her next novel, Lindsey spends her time reading, wandering through the foothills around her house, and planning her future hobby farm. She lives in the Pacific Northwest with her rather confused cats.

www.LindseyFairleigh.com

19987678R00132

Printed in Great Britain
by Amazon